RIDE THE WAVE

HER ELEMENTAL DRAGONS BOOK FOUR

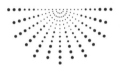

ELIZABETH BRIGGS

Cover Designed by Andreea Vraciu

ISBN (paperback) 9781795735834

ISBN (ebook) 978-1-948456-04-3

www.elizabethbriggs.net

For all the parents trying to make the world a better place

1

JASIN

I glared at the man in front of me with his all-too-familiar hazel eyes. Doran, the Azure Dragon, was one of the men I'd spent months training to defeat. It was my destiny to help overthrow him and the rest of the Black Dragon's mates to restore balance to the world. They'd only brought chaos, misery, and death to the four Realms, and now they'd kidnapped the woman I loved. I wanted to rip his head off, set fire to his body, and watch his bones turn to ash, but I couldn't—because he'd just told us he was Kira's father.

Doran had the tanned, weathered skin of a man who spent his days in the sun, and his long sandy hair was wind-tossed and a little wild. While Isen, the Golden Dragon, had the bearing of a prince, and Sark and Heldor, the Crimson Dragon and the Jade Dragon, were obviously warriors, Doran looked more like a sailor or a pirate, especially with his scruffy beard, plain white shirt, black trousers and boots.

I wasn't fooled by his appearance though. The man was dangerous, and he was our enemy.

"Why should we believe anything you say?" I asked, while my hand lingered on the hilt of my sword and fire burned inside me, begging to be released. Slade and Auric tensed beside me, ready to join me if things turned ugly. We stood in the ruins of the Earth Temple surrounded by shimmering crystals on the stone walls, a broken Dragon statue, and two bodies on the ground. One of them was Reven's.

Doran held up his hands as if in surrender. "I realize you have no reason to trust me, but Kira's life is in danger and we need to rescue her before it's too late."

"You knocked her out and carried her away, but now you want to rescue her?" Slade asked, his voice a low growl. His green eyes were hard as stone and a thin layer of sweat coated his dark skin despite the chill in the air. He'd been unable to stop Kira from being kidnapped, only minutes after he'd completed the bonding with her that allowed him to turn into a Dragon, and it obviously weighed heavily on him.

Auric's gray eyes flashed with anger. "If you're her father why would you kidnap her in the first place, knowing it would put her life in danger?"

"Kira was obviously going to be captured one way or another," Doran said. "I took matters into my own hands to make sure she wasn't injured in the process. The others would not be as careful with her life as I was."

"You could have helped us stop them," Slade said, crossing his thick, muscular arms.

"Perhaps, but I'm not ready for Nysa or the others to know my true loyalties yet. The Black Dragon still trusts me, which allows me a great advantage." Doran's eyes narrowed. "But I won't let my daughter be killed either. I've spent my entire life protecting her and making sure the other Dragons never found her. I'm not about to stop now."

My fingers still hovered near the hilt of my sword despite his words. I wanted to believe him, but we had no reason to trust anything he said. "I don't like this," I said to Slade and Auric. "For all we know he could be leading us into a trap."

"I could be," Doran agreed. "But you're never going to be able to rescue Kira without my help. Especially with one of your men down."

Reven's body was encased in a thin layer of ice, the only thing keeping him alive after the Dragon attack. Beneath the ice, his black hair was thick with dried blood, and his side was horribly burned. He'd sacrificed himself to protect Kira, and her magic was the only thing that could heal him. By saving her, we'd be saving him too.

Unfortunately, we couldn't save the life of the man lying beside Reven. Parin had been the leader of the Resistance and despite his uncomfortable past with Slade, he'd led Kira and the others to the Earth Temple. He'd died trying to protect Kira from the Dragons, and he'd be remembered as a hero once this was all over.

Auric ran a hand through his short blond hair, his face pinched. "I don't trust Doran either, but he has a point. Without our bond it could take us a long time to find Kira."

At his words, I searched for Kira again and found only emptiness. Ever since I'd bonded with Kira at the Fire Temple, I could feel her presence, but something was blocking me now. Somehow the Black Dragon was making sure we couldn't find her.

"Tell us where she's being held," Slade demanded, squaring his broad shoulders as he faced down the Azure Dragon. "Then we'll decide whether or not we need your help."

"She's in Soulspire," Doran said, naming the capital of the four Realms, where the Black Dragon ruled with her mates. "Inside a secret part of the palace."

Damn. He was right that rescuing Kira would be nearly impossible for us. I'd been to Soulspire once, back when I was a soldier in the Onyx Army, and the palace was heavily guarded. Not to mention, the other Dragons would be there, and we weren't yet a match for them. Having Doran on our side could tilt the balance toward us, but I still wasn't convinced this wasn't a trick. For all we knew he was luring us to our own deaths or to a prison cell beside Kira's.

"What's your plan exactly?" I asked. If he told us how to rescue her, perhaps we'd be able to accomplish it without his help. "Do you even have one?"

Doran gave me an amused look. "I'm not that much of a fool. If I tell you my plan now—and yes, I do have one— you'll rush ahead without me, and then you'll all be dead. Not that I care, but Kira needs you alive."

Well, it was worth a try.

He spread his hands. "Listen, I can't prove to you that

I'm her father or that I'd do anything to protect her. All you have is my word, and my promise that if we do nothing, Kira will be dead within a few days."

Auric glanced between me and Slade. "As much as I hate to admit it, I don't think we have a choice. We need to work with him, even if it is a trap."

"If it's a trap, we'll be ready," I said, slamming my fist into my other palm. "But what are we going to do with Reven? We can't leave him here in the ruins of the Earth Temple."

"We could stop by the Resistance hideout on the way and leave Reven with them," Auric said. "He'd be safe there, and we can return Parin's body at the same time so they can bury him."

"No," Slade said immediately. "We can't lead Doran to the Resistance. I won't put all those lives in danger by revealing their location to a Dragon."

Doran chuckled. "No need to worry about that. I already know where it is. They're in the mountain by the two rocks that look like breasts."

"How do you know?" I asked.

"I'm the Black Dragon's...scout, you could say. It's my job to know these things and many more. But don't worry, I haven't shared this information with Nysa or the other Dragons yet. I have no interest in seeing the Resistance wiped out."

Slade scowled at him while Auric looked thoughtful. I tried to come up with another place where we could leave Reven, but all I could think of was Slade's village, except

5

we'd put all those innocent people in danger too. I briefly considered leaving Reven with Auric's father, the King of the Air Realm, but Stormhaven was too far out of the way and time was of the essence. Taking Reven to the Resistance hideout was our best option.

Doran rolled his shoulders and turned toward the tunnel that led out of here. "Enough debating. I don't know how much longer the Black Dragon will keep Kira alive. Right now, Kira is an amusement, but she's a threat to Nysa's rule and will have to be eliminated soon. We need to get moving."

"There's one more problem," I said, rubbing the spot on my back that hurt even in my human form. "Auric is the only one of us who can fly at the moment. One of my wings is busted, and Slade just got his Dragon form a few hours ago."

Doran shrugged. "That's not an issue. Someone can ride with me."

Ride on the back of our enemy? As if this day couldn't get any worse.

2

KIRA

I woke to pain. The bone cage surrounded me, cutting off my bond with my mates and blocking my powers. Every time my bare skin touched one of the white bars, revulsion and horror filled me. I'd tried to stay awake, but after being left here for untold hours exhaustion had finally taken over. Except I could only sleep upright without bringing on waves of disgust, and my back and neck ached from the uncomfortable position. Even worse, every now and then my head would drop to the side, my cheek would brush against one of the dreaded bones, and I'd nearly empty my stomach.

A noise caught my attention and jerked me fully awake. A footstep on the stone floor. Heavy. Probably male. Not my mother then.

The Black Dragon had only come to visit me once, and since then I'd been left alone. I wasn't sure how long I'd been locked in this prison, or whether it was day or night.

The room that held my bone cage was empty except for a single torch, with no windows and only one door. After my mother's cryptic words that I wouldn't be alive much longer, I'd tried to summon my powers of earth, air, and fire, but found I couldn't use them in here. Without my magic or my weapons, I wasn't sure how I'd ever escape, but I was determined to not let this be the end.

The door opened, and my worst nightmare stood in the doorway. Sark, the Crimson Dragon, who had once murdered the people I'd called my parents. I knew now that the Black Dragon was my true mother and one of her Dragons was my father. Probably Sark himself, although the thought made me feel sicker than touching the bones did.

But Sark's crimes didn't end there. He'd murdered Reven's family too, he'd helped destroy the town I'd lived in for the last few years, and he'd killed my best friend, Tash. He'd taken so much from me and from the people I cared for, and I wanted nothing more than to defeat him and stop him from hurting anyone else.

He strode into the room and the torch beside him flared brighter, illuminating his nearly white hair, which was cut in a short military style. He wore red and black armor, similar to what the Onyx Army wore, but even more ornate. Hatred filled me as he drew closer and his cruel brown eyes met mine. He carried a tray of food, which he thrust through the bone cage with a single command. "Eat."

My stomach twisted with hunger, even as I glared at him. The last time I'd eaten had been during the climb to the Earth Temple with Slade, Reven, and Parin. How long ago was that? It felt like an eternity, but for all I knew it had only been a few hours. Were my mates all right? Were they looking for me now?

The tray smelled heavenly and was piled high with roasted chicken, carrots, and potatoes, along with a pitcher of water. I considered whether the food and water might be poisoned, but quickly dismissed the idea. My gifts from the Spirit Goddess would probably heal me from any poison, and the Dragons could have killed me instead of locking me up. No, they wanted me alive...for now. They must have a plan if they were feeding me, but what?

"Take it," Sark said, thrusting the tray forward again.

My resolve failed, and I snatched the tray out of his hands, making sure not to touch him. I retreated to the back of my cage and began to pick at the food, while he crossed his arms and watched me the entire time I ate. Hunger quickly took over and I began to devour the food under his dreadful gaze like an animal trapped in a cage, waiting to be turned into a meal. All they had to do was fatten me up first.

When I finished, I threw the empty tray through the bars of my cage at him. He dodged it easily with a grunt, picked it up off the floor, and turned to walk away. Fury rose up in me and I called out, "Why are you keeping me here? What do you want?"

He left the room without answering me, the door slamming shut and locking behind him. With anger fueling me, I wrapped my hands around the bone cage and shook it hard. That heavy revulsion and nausea filled me, but I held on for as long as I could and used all my strength to try to pry a

9

bone loose. Nothing budged. I was forced to let go, staggering back as sweat dripped down my forehead and bile clung to my throat.

There would be no breaking through this cage.

For a few minutes I had to focus on breathing in and out to make sure I didn't bring up the food I'd just eaten. When I no longer felt sick, I sighed and slowly sank to the floor. My head fell forward into my hands and I rubbed my temples, unsure if I wanted to scream or cry. I couldn't escape, I had no idea if my mates were alive or dead, and all I could do was wait and pray for a way out.

Where was Enva? She usually came to me when I was upset, and I could use my grandmother's advice now more than ever. Perhaps the bone cage was preventing her from manifesting too?

One thing was certain: I was truly all alone here.

3

SLADE

The journey to the Resistance hideout in the mountains was tense. None of us trusted Doran or wanted anything to do with him, but one of us had to ride on his back, so I'd volunteered. I considered it my penance for letting Kira be kidnapped. What good was being a Dragon now if I couldn't actually fly? Kira was captured, Reven was in a coma, and Parin was dead—all because of me. Nothing I did could ever make up for my failures, but the least I could do was return Parin's body to the Resistance and then prepare to rescue Kira.

As the Earth Realm soared below me, I tried to quench the fear and unease that came with being so far above the earth. Without my feet on solid ground I never felt comfortable, not since the Earth God had blessed me with his favor and his powers. That blessing now seemed to be holding me back. Would I ever be able to fly? Or would I be useless as a Dragon forever?

Doran set down in the forest while Auric—with Jasin and Reven on his back—landed at the Resistance base's secret entrance in the mountain. We'd decided it would be better for everyone if the Resistance didn't know we were working with Doran, for fear it would cause a panic or provoke an attack. We needed him, no matter how much we hated it.

A short while later, Auric returned and collected us, along with Parin's body. With Doran's commonplace clothes and his hooded cloak covering much of his face, no one recognized him when we entered the Resistance hideout. I wasn't surprised, since he was rarely seen in his human form, especially in the Earth Realm. Besides, no one expected a Dragon to look more like a carefree drifter than one of the men who ruled our world through fear and death.

As we stepped into the smooth caves of the hideout, we were greeted by an older woman named Daka who we'd met once before. We'd rescued her and a few other people from the Onyx Army in the Fire Realm before they could be executed for being members of the Resistance.

"It's a blessing to see you've returned," Daka said. Her brown hair was streaked with gray and her skin was tanned and wrinkled, but her eyes shone bright. "Please come in and we'll get you settled. You must be exhausted."

"It's good to see you made it to the Resistance base alive," I said.

"Yes, thanks to you." She smiled, but then her smile fell

when she noticed our dwindled numbers and the two life-less bodies we'd brought with us.

"I wish we were here under better circumstances," Auric said. "Unfortunately, Kira has been kidnapped, one of our men is in a coma, and Parin... He gave his life fighting the Dragons. I'm sorry."

Daka covered her mouth as she let out a soft cry, her eyes filling with tears. "Oh, Parin, no. What will we do without him leading us? And with Faya gone too..."

Her tears reminded me of my failure, and I looked away, focusing on the hidden town of Slateden behind her. The stone and wooden buildings stood below the high, domed ceiling of the cave, but the roads were nearly empty today. Most of the Resistance members had left to fight the battle at Salt Creek Tower and wouldn't return for another week, including my sister, Leni. Auric and Jasin had assured me she was alive when they last saw her, but I would continue to worry until I saw her with my own eyes.

Auric stood up straighter, though his voice was weary. "I'll bring Faya back. She's needed here now."

I rested a hand on Auric's shoulder. He'd already flown across the Earth Realm for hours with no break, and now he was preparing to set out again. The man had to be exhausted, and I respected him more than ever. "And my sister?"

He nodded. "Don't worry. I'll get her and Brin too."

I nearly hugged the man. "Thank you."

"I should be going with you," Jasin grumbled, the frustration clear in his brown eyes. "Stupid wing. Make sure you eat something before you go."

"I will," Auric said, as they clasped each other in a quick hug. The two of them were like brothers now, which was still hard to believe, considering they'd once hated each other.

As Daka took Auric away to find some food, Jasin sighed. "I wish I could do more."

I knew exactly how he felt.

Sleep proved elusive that night. I tossed and turned, worrying about Kira, praying my sister was unharmed, and hating myself for my failures. When the sun began to rise, I gave up, threw off my blankets, and went to find some food.

I nearly crashed into my youngest sister in the entrance to the guest house, along with her girlfriend, Brin. Relief flooded me as I swept Leni into my arms. She was the most headstrong, stubborn, and frustrating woman in our family, but she was alive and that was all that mattered. She and Brin had joined the Resistance in the battle at Salt Creek Tower, even though she was too young and inexperienced as a fighter, in my opinion. I wished she was back at home and safe with our mother and sister in Clayridge, but she was an adult and didn't listen to her overprotective brother anymore, much to my dismay.

"Slade!" she said as she embraced me back.

I pulled back to look her over, my grip tight on her arms. Her dark skin was smudged with dirt and some of her small braids were starting to come undone, but she appeared to be well otherwise. "Are you unharmed?"

"Yes, I'm fine. I twisted my ankle, but it's already better." She glanced over my shoulder with a smile. "Brin had my back."

I turned toward Brin and bowed my head. "Thank you."

With golden skin and silky black hair, Brin was beautiful and had the grace of a woman born to money and power, although she was an excellent fighter too. She was a noblewoman from the Air Realm and had once been Auric's fiancé, though they'd never been more than friends. I just hoped she wouldn't break my sister's heart.

She gave me a dazzling smile. "I would never allow any harm to come to Leni, and she protected me as well."

"I did what I could." Leni nudged me in the side with a grin. "So is it done? Did you and Kira get intimate? Are you a Dragon now?"

My shoulders tensed. It was bad enough talking to my sister about "getting intimate." It was worse being reminded of my failure. "Yes, we bonded and I'm a Dragon now, although I'm still not used to it. But we were attacked by the other Dragons, and Kira was taken. I... I couldn't stop them."

Leni squeezed my arm. "I'm sure you did the best you could."

"Tell us everything," Brin said.

I gave them the quick rundown of what happened, although I didn't mention that Doran was helping us. In return, they told me about the battle at Salt Creek Tower with the Dragons. By the end of their tale they were both yawning, and I guessed they had been up all night as they flew here on Auric's back.

I sent them both to get some rest, and then caught sight of a beautiful, dark-skinned woman with short hair on the street outside the guest house. Faya's head was bent and her eyes were red, but her back was straight as she walked alone. I headed outside to speak with the woman I once thought I'd marry.

"I'm sorry about Parin," I said. "He died a hero and fulfilled his duty to the Earth God. We would not have found the Earth Temple without him."

Faya nodded. "His mother would be proud. Thank you for bringing his body back to us so that we may bury him."

"It was the least we could do to honor his sacrifice." I touched her arm. "I truly am sorry, Faya. What will you do now?"

She gazed down the empty streets of Slateden, her face a mixture of grief and grim determination. "The Resistance still needs a leader. I will step up and do what I can until they can elect someone else. It's what Parin would have wanted."

"You'll make a good leader."

"I doubt I could ever be the leader Parin was, but I'll do my best." Her hand rested on her lower stomach. "Not only for his sake or the Resistance's, but for his child."

I stepped back, my eyes dropping to her waist. "You're pregnant?"

"Yes, I'm three months along. We tried for years without success and never thought it would happen. Now he won't get to see our child born." She sighed and her body sagged, all the energy leaving her small frame. "At least a part of him will live on."

I wrapped my arms around her and clasped her in a warm embrace. She buried her face in my chest for a few moments, allowing me to lend her my strength, before pulling away. Over the years, Faya had been my lover, my enemy, and now my ally. We'd been through a lot together and our shared history would always be a part of us. Until recently I'd wanted nothing to do with her, but now I only wished the best for her and her child.

"I heard you're leaving soon to rescue Kira," she said. "Take whatever supplies you need for your journey."

"Thank you. Please watch over Reven for us until we return."

"We will. No harm will come to him, I swear it."

We said our goodbyes and I returned to my room in the hopes of getting a few more hours of sleep before our journey. Gods knew I would need it to face what was ahead.

4

KIRA

I waited in my cage for an eternity with only a bucket in
the corner, a torn and dirty blanket, and whatever food
and water the Dragons brought me. The bucket was a gift
from Heldor, who came to see me after Sark. His face was
solemn as he gave it to me, and thankfully he didn't wait
around to watch me use it to relieve myself. Isen brought me
the blanket some time later, though he warned me not to get
too comfortable because I wouldn't be there very long. I
could only imagine what Doran would gift me with when he
came to visit me next.

When the door opened again some time later it wasn't
Doran who stepped inside, but Nysa. In an instant it
became hard to breathe, my entire body tensing with anticipation and dread at the sight of her. My mother was incredibly beautiful, with an ageless quality I'd only seen before in
the other Dragons. Her hair was the same red shade as mine

and hung in luxurious waves to her shoulders, but her eyes were the color of emeralds. She had the kind of beauty that would turn every head in a crowd, even if she hadn't been the most feared woman in the world.

"Good morning, Kira," she said, as the door shut behind her and she approached the cage.

Was it morning? I couldn't tell. How many days had I been here now?

"How are you feeling?" she asked, her voice pleasant. She wore a long white and black gown that trailed along the floor behind her with each graceful step, and it was impossible not to stare at her.

I ignored her question. "What do you want with me?"

She stopped a few inches from the cage and clasped her hands in front of her. "I need to take your life. Believe me, it's not something I want to do, but it's what must be done."

"Then kill me already! Why wait?"

"It's not that simple." She tilted her head as she studied me from head to toe. "You must understand, I do not want you to die. If it were up to me, we would rule together as mother and daughter."

My fists clenched at my side. "I have no interest in ruling, and certainly not with you."

She waved her hand dismissively. "Your view of me is distorted by what others have told you. The truth is that everything I do is meant to protect this world. Including your sacrifice."

A hard lump formed in my throat. "Sacrifice?"

"Unfortunately, yes." She let out a long sigh. "I will

drain your life force, and it will keep me and my mates young until my next daughter is born."

Horror and revulsion filled me, even stronger than when I'd touched the bone cage. "Your *next* one?"

"I do have to apologize," Nysa continued, as if she hadn't heard me. "This would be a lot easier for all of us if you were still a baby, like the others before you. Now you've bonded with some of your mates and I must take extra precautions since you won't be drained so easily. Of course, it also means your strength will become mine, making me even more powerful." She dipped her head. "I will do my best to honor your sacrifice."

All I could do was stare at her with my mouth hanging open as I absorbed everything she said, along with the implications. When the Gods created the five Dragons they were only supposed to be in power for a short time before being replaced by their daughter and her mates, beginning the cycle anew. All of that ended with Nysa, and I'd never known why. Until now. "That's how you've lived so long. You drain the life from your own children."

"I have no other choice."

I'd always thought she was a monster, but I'd had no idea how dark her soul truly was. How many of my sisters had died before me to keep her immortal? How many babies had she drained to keep herself young?

"Oh, Kira." She reached for me through the cage and I jerked back. She wrapped her hands around the bars instead, untouched by the revulsion that always struck me.

"If I could save you, I would. But this is the only way to contain her."

"Who?"

My mother gave me a sad, lovely smile before stepping back. "The Spirit Goddess."

I could only stare at her as she left the room. Why would she want to contain the Spirit Goddess? We were descended from the Spirit Goddess and had been given her powers. The other Gods of Fire, Earth, Air, and Water were all her mates, and they'd tasked us with protecting the world. We'd been given our own mates to help us accomplish this task, and the Dragons were meant to serve the Gods and carry out their will—except Nysa and her Dragons seemed to be the enemies of the Gods instead. I'd assumed it was because Nysa had refused to give up her power, but maybe there was more to it?

It didn't matter. Nysa was evil, power hungry, and completely insane. She had to be in order to murder her own children to extend her life. She'd said she had a good reason and was trying to protect the world, but I didn't believe it. Nothing could make me do that to my own child. *Nothing.* Nysa was a monster, a mother who sucked the life from her own babies, and no matter how much she said she didn't want to kill me, no one was forcing her to do it. And she'd made the same decision many times before.

The horror over what Nysa had done—and wanted to do to me—suffocated me, and I became consumed with the need to get away. I grabbed the bucket off the floor and slammed it against the cage as hard as I could. I did it over and over, the metal hitting the bone loudly with each blow, hoping for something to give way. Just one little piece. *Please*, I prayed to the Gods, *give me a way to escape from here. Let me free, so I might find a way to stop her.*

The door flew open and Sark stomped inside the room. "What's going on in here?"

I dropped the bucket and glared at him, while my entire body shook with anger and disgust. "How could you let her do it? She's killing your own children, and you stood there and allowed it for all these years!"

His lips curled up in a sneer. "Stupid girl. You don't know anything."

"I know a real father would protect his daughter," I spat out.

"Sometimes sacrifices must be made for the greater good. Now quit your banging or I'll take that bucket away, along with everything else you've been allowed."

I gave him a look full of hatred and loathing as I picked up the bucket and banged it against the cage, making the bones rattle. Maybe if he tried to take the bucket, I'd be able to overpower him and escape. It wasn't a great plan, but it was better than nothing and I was desperate at this point.

But he didn't open the cage or come after me. Instead, the metal bucket suddenly grew so hot that I yelped and was forced to drop it. Sark had used his fire magic through the cage somehow, even though I couldn't use mine.

"Be quiet, or next time it won't only be the bucket getting burned," he growled.

After he left, I realized he hadn't confirmed or denied

being my father. The bucket hadn't done a single thing to the bone cage, and I had nothing else to use to escape besides a ragged blanket. But I wouldn't give up. I couldn't. Somehow, I would get out of here—and then I would make sure that none of my sisters would ever be killed again.

5

AURIC

O ur cart pulled up to the black gates of Soulspire and
I shifted in my seat, tugging my wide-brimmed hat
low over my face. We'd bought the cart at a farm a few hours
away, along with clothes that would help us blend in and
look like merchants, plus some apples and oranges to
complete our disguise. The farmer had been delighted with
our money and I was thankful my father had provided us so
much gold for our journey before we'd left the Air Realm. It
was almost all gone now, but it had served us well while it
lasted.

We hadn't seen Doran since his large blue form had
flown over us toward the palace. We could only pray he was
getting Kira out and fulfilling his side of the bargain,
instead of leading us into a trap. I had a feeling he would be
true to his word, even if the others disagreed with me. Or
maybe I just wanted to believe Doran was on our side

because if he wasn't, we would have a much harder time rescuing Kira.

We'd spent the last few days flying toward Soulspire, which was located in the center of the continent where the four Realms met, and Doran had told us his plan when we'd stopped to rest last night.

"The Spirit Festival starts tomorrow, and it's the biggest celebration of the year in Soulspire," he'd said. "The Black Dragon herself always makes a speech in the afternoon and the revelers will fill the streets, wearing masks and celebrating being alive. It can get a bit wild, if you know what I mean. It's the perfect time to rescue Kira."

"And how exactly will we do that?" Slade asked. We all sat around a clearing as we finished our meal, and despite having traveled with Doran for days, everyone kept an eye on him. None of us trusted him yet.

"You won't," Doran said. "I will."

"That doesn't work for us," Jasin growled. He disliked the man more than any of us, although I wasn't sure if it was a natural fire and water opposites thing or if it was related to his issues with his own parents. Jasin's father had betrayed us, and I didn't blame him for suspecting Kira's father would do the same.

Doran gave a casual shrug. "Too bad. I'm the only one who can walk into the palace where Kira is being held without a problem. Any one of you would be stopped by the hundreds of guards and killed or captured before you came anywhere near her. Assuming you could even find her once inside." He shook his head. "No, I will free Kira and lead her out of the palace through the sewers. You'll meet me there and escape with her."

"Why do you need us at all then?" Jasin asked.

"I can get Kira out of the palace while the other Dragons are busy with the Festival, but they'd notice if I flew off with her. I need it to look like she was rescued by her mates to maintain my cover."

Jasin's eyes narrowed, and I held out a hand to stop him from replying. I cleared my throat. "How will we get into the city undetected? You can fly into Soulspire, but we cannot."

Doran ran a hand over his beard. "Many people will be traveling to the city for the festival, especially merchants and performers. If you look convincing enough, they'll let you in without a problem. Trust me, no one will be looking for you. They'll be celebrating life in every way they can." Doran smirked. "Let's just say a lot of babies are born in Soulspire nine months from now."

We hammered out the rest of the details as we ate. None of us liked that Doran would be getting Kira out alone, but we couldn't think of a good way to get into the palace ourselves.

Sneaking into the capital proved to be easy though. It had been my idea to buy the cart and pretend to be farmers selling our wares, and as the gates opened and the guards gestured for us to enter, our disguise seemed to be working. Slade snapped the reins and our horses pulled us forward into the city.

I'd been to Soulspire twice before. Once as a young

child, which I barely remembered, and a second time when I was older, perhaps about twelve. My father had taken me and my brother Garet with him while he attended to some business with Isen. All I remembered was the gleaming black palace looming over me and the claustrophobic feel of being surrounded by Onyx Army soldiers watching our every move.

Both of those things still existed today, except the city had been transformed from the somber, imposing one of my memories to a chaotic, festive, and colorful splendor. Banners and flags hung from every building, splashing the black architecture with a rainbow of colors. Every street was crowded with people in their finest clothes, wearing intricate masks that covered much of their faces, except their lips —which many used quite generously on each other. Most of the masks resembled animals, while others were decorated with flowers and leaves, all to honor the Spirit Goddess.

As we continued through the city, the crowd made it difficult to maneuver the cart toward the location of the sewer entrance. Alcohol and food flowed freely, music burst out of packed taverns and cafes, and people danced and threw confetti in the streets. Others were sharing kisses or locked in intimate embraces, their hands wandering under skirts and inside trousers, and I could see what Doran meant by it getting a little wild today.

A longing for Kira tugged at my soul, but when I reached for her through our bond, I still found nothing. I hadn't realized how vital feeling her in the back of my mind had become, but now it was as if a piece of myself was missing. I couldn't sense Jasin or Slade either, not without Kira acting as the bridge between us, but at least they were here beside me.

"I think this is it." Slade stopped the cart outside some stone steps that led down to an arched metal door. A guard stood in front of the sewer entrance, wearing the scaled black armor and winged helmet of the Onyx Army.

I nodded. "It matches the description Doran gave us."

Jasin quickly knocked out the guard and dragged him through the door, which Slade opened with his magic. Once the guard was tied up, we left him there and continued forward. Jasin created a ball of flame to illuminate the dark tunnel that surrounded us, made of black stone with low domed ceilings that our heads nearly reached. A terrible smell lingered in the air, and we walked through ankle-deep water and Gods only knew what else. The tunnels were old and in some sections the water was deeper, leaving us no choice but to wade through it. I cringed to think of what my clothes would smell like when we got out of the place.

"Where's Reven when we need him?" Jasin muttered, as we dipped into a waist-high patch of murky water.

Slade pressed his hand against a slimy wall and closed his eyes, using his magic to spread his senses through the earth. "This tunnel leads up to the palace. How far are we supposed to go to meet them?"

"I'm not sure," I said. "I suppose we should keep walking until we see them."

Jasin snorted. "If they're even coming."

I opened my mouth to reply when I spotted something

up ahead. Tiny pinpricks of dim light that looked a lot like a pair of eyes. I immediately reached for my two long knives, which had been a gift from my father.

Jasin made his fire flare brighter, casting light across the tunnel and illuminating six shadowy figures with long claws. They seemed to be made of darkness itself, their bodies disappearing into the gloom where their feet should be, except for those sickly yellow glowing eyes.

"Shades!" I called out, as I reached for my magic and sheathed my blades. Shades were once thought to be myth, but we'd fought them before at the Air Temple and now knew they worked for the Black Dragon. Shades could drain the life of anyone they touched and were immune to most weapons, but magic could hurt them. The Black Dragon must have left them here to stop anyone from entering the palace this way, though it seemed dangerous to have so many in the middle of the capital. Maybe she kept them here in case she ever needed to unleash them across Soulspire.

We all stepped forward and prepared to attack, gathering our magic around us. I tapped into the unseen currents of air that floated around us at all times and sensed the quick breathing of my companions. The air here was damp and polluted with foul smells and toxins, but it still served me.

I slammed the shades with a huge blast of wind, knocking them all into the wall of the tunnel. Slade caused the stone there to grab hold of the shades, imprisoning them while they let out spine-tingling shrieks, and then Jasin incinerated them one by one.

"That was a lot easier than I remember it being at the Air Temple," Jasin said, as the shades turned to smoke.

I grinned. "We've had a lot more practice using our magic and working as a team."

"Wait," Slade said, holding out his arm to stop us from moving forward.

Dozens of glowing eyes lit up the tunnel ahead of us, blocking our path. I counted at least twenty pairs before giving up, and more seemed to fill the tunnel every second. I swallowed hard and prepared to fight them, while Slade and Jasin did the same. If we were going to get Kira out safely, we'd have to defeat them all.

6

KIRA

The door to my cell opened, jerking me awake. A tall man stood in the doorway, dimly lit by the dying embers of the torch outside my cage. I recognized his long blond hair and tanned skin—the Azure Dragon. I was wondering when he would show up. The others had been by at least twice now.

I'd seen Doran three times before. The first was a year after my parents were killed by Sark. I'd been traveling with some merchants and we'd stopped in a small town in the Air Realm. He'd shifted to his human form and spoke with one of the merchants, while his cold eyes searched around as if he was looking for someone. I left the merchants the next morning, worried I was putting their lives at risk. Much later, I saw Doran fly over the Earth Realm after I'd met my mates, and we'd hidden while his huge dragon form had circled over us before finally leaving.

The last time I saw him was when he'd kidnapped me a few days ago.

I saw a bundle in his hands and wondered what he'd brought to pacify me until my life was sucked away to keep him and the others alive. I still wasn't sure why they bothered, honestly. Maybe they really were fattening me up like a pig they prepared to slaughter.

"We don't have much time." Doran said, as he approached my cage. He offered me a bar of soap and a wet wash cloth in one hand, with a bundle of fabric in the other. "Get clean and change into these clothes as quickly as you can."

I frowned as I took the items from him and watched his back as he left the room. After untold days in the same clothes I'd worn in the Earth Temple I was eager to change into something new and be moderately clean again, but the fact that Doran had brought me this now probably meant my time was up. They were getting me ready for my sacrifice, I was sure of it.

The dress he'd given me only reinforced that theory. It was a long gown made of the finest velvet in a deep green, trimmed in silver and adorned with intricate designs across the bodice. A long, hooded cloak in dark gray completed the ensemble, and he'd even brought me some clean undergarments too. I supposed they wanted me to look beautiful for them when they drained my life.

I sighed and washed myself as best I could before changing into the new clothes. Once I was done, some of the haze from the days spent in the cage seemed to lift. Being clean and wearing a fresh set of clothes made me feel like a human being again instead of an animal trapped in a cage. And if they thought I would go easily to my own sacrifice they were in for a surprise.

Doran entered the room again and his gaze quickly swept over me. "Good, you're ready." He unlocked the bone cage with a key I'd never seen before. "Now follow me and do everything I say. We'll need to hurry."

Why he thought I'd hurry to my own death was a mystery, but then again, the Dragons were all very odd. In the brief snippets of conversation I'd shared with the others they'd spoken as if I should be honored they were going to kill me.

The cage opened and I stumbled out of it. The second I was past the bones, energy rushed through me, as if I'd taken a breath after being underwater too long. My magic filled me with power and reconnected me to my mates. I sensed Jasin and Auric immediately, like bright sparks in my consciousness, and relief made me nearly laugh out loud. Slade was there too, a cool, reassuring presence in my mind, but our connection was still new and not as strong.

They were close. Were they coming to rescue me?

For the first time in days I had hope, and I channeled it as I reached for Auric and Jasin's magic, combining it and gathering it in my palms. I turned toward Doran and with a bellow of rage I launched a lightning bolt at him. It struck his chest and threw him back against the wall, knocking him out with a sizzling sound.

I'd never done that before. During training I'd been able

to summon lightning for only a second and it had been little more than a spark, even though Jasin and Auric had been able to master it. But my determination to get out of here and find my mates again made me stronger, and nothing was getting in the way of my escape.

I threw open the cell door and started to rush out, but a strong hand grasped my shoulder and yanked me back.

"What do you think you're doing?" Doran asked, clutching his chest where I'd struck him.

I jerked away and gathered fire around me like a shield. "I won't let you take me!"

"Take you?" He stepped back from the flames and rolled his eyes. "I'm trying to help you escape!"

"You...what?"

"I'm here with your mates. They're waiting outside." He held out his hand and offered me a small black mask covered in twirling dark green vines. "Put this on and we'll go to them."

I plucked the mask from his hand and stared at it. "Why would you help me?"

"Kira, I'm your father."

The floor seemed to fall out from under me and I staggered back. My first thought was, *thank the Gods it isn't Sark.* The doubt came next, but as he held my eyes, I realized they were a mirror of my own. I took him in slowly and caught other similarities in our features too. He truly was my father.

And not a very good one.

Fire flared around me. "You knocked me out and kidnapped me!"

"To protect you!" He sighed and dragged a hand through his long sandy hair. "I'll explain everything later, I promise. Right now we really need to get out of here before anyone notices us. We have a small window while Nysa and the others are busy, but it will only last so long, and we don't have much time to meet your mates."

"Where are they? Are they all okay?"

"Put on your mask and follow me. I'll take you to them."

I donned the mask, snapping it over my head. "Why the mask?"

"Today is the Spirit Festival. The entire city is wearing masks. It's the perfect time to escape Soulspire." Doran put his own mask on, which featured tiny brightly colored fish, before stepping out of the room into a dark corridor. He scanned the length of it before setting off, clutching his side where I'd injured him. I wasn't sorry. He deserved it, even if he was helping me—which I wasn't positive he was.

I drew in a long breath, quickly weighed my options, and then followed him. If this was a trick, I'd fight back with everything I had, but I couldn't stay in that prison one more second.

The corridor was empty and had a musty smell with no windows, making me wonder if we were underground. I hadn't realized we were in Soulspire, although I'd suspected it. I'd never been to the capital before, and I was beginning to realize that without Doran's help I might never have made it out on my own. Assuming he was truly helping me now and not leading me to my death.

We walked with quick purposeful strides and I fell in step beside him, although my limbs were stiff from being in a cage for so long and my muscles were weak from inactivity. As we continued through the long stone halls, we passed a few guards, who stood up straight and nodded at Doran. They completely ignored my presence, and I had a feeling it was only because I was at his side.

"Where are we?" I asked in a low voice.

"The lower levels of the palace," Doran said. "Keep moving."

That burst of energy when I'd exited the cage had begun to fade, and now a bone-deep exhaustion was beginning to set in. I pushed past it and kept moving, fueled by the knowledge that I would see my mates again soon.

Doran stopped at an unmarked door and opened it, then gestured for me to enter. All I saw was darkness and a putrid smell hit my nose. I gagged and stepped back, but Doran shoved me forward through the door. He slammed it shut behind us and I quickly summoned a flame to fight back the darkness.

We were in a domed tunnel of some sort, with a thin trickle of water running down the center of it. Doran grabbed a torch off the wall and lit it with the fire in my palm, then gestured for me to follow him. "Your mates are waiting for us in these sewers. Once we find them, they'll get you out of the city."

"You're not coming?" I asked.

"No, I still have work to do here, but I promise I'll find you later. I've waited a long time to be reunited with you and we have a lot to talk about."

I gave him a skeptical look as we began walking down the dark tunnel. He'd had twenty years to find me, and Gods knew I could have used his advice and help during the last few months. Or after Sark killed my family. Or any of the other times I'd found myself on the run or in danger. It was difficult to believe he'd suddenly become a loving father now, when he'd been absent all these years. And why was I any different from my sisters, who he'd allowed to be murdered for centuries?

I didn't trust him one bit and I had a million questions for him, but I also recognized he was my only hope of getting out of here. I followed him down the tunnels despite my hesitations, but as soon as we had a chance to talk, I would need some answers.

The moment I saw a familiar broad-shouldered frame ahead of me, I let out a loud cry and stumbled forward. "Slade!"

He turned toward me, and his eyes widened. He crossed the distance between us with a few steps and swept me up into his arms. I laughed and sobbed at the same time, so relieved to be in his arms again.

"Kira!" Jasin called out, but he was busy holding off five shades with Auric at his side.

Doran gestured idly and each of the shades turned to ice, then broke apart into a million pieces. Gods, he was powerful. It was a grim reminder that we still had a lot to learn to match the other Dragons' strength.

As the shades vanished, my other mates rushed forward to wrap me in their arms and sprinkle my face with kisses. I was overjoyed to be united with them again and to see with my own eyes they were safe.

But then I realized one person was missing.

"Where's Reven?" I asked, suddenly worried.

Each of their faces darkened. "He's injured," Auric said. "But now that you're free, you can heal him."

"*What?*" My heart pounded and panic gripped my throat.

"There's no time to explain," Doran said. "Take Kira and get her out of the city. I'll meet you back at the Resistance base in a few days."

Wait, Doran knew about the Resistance base? My head spun as I tried to take everything in, realizing I'd missed a lot while I'd been captured. I was desperate to know what happened to Reven and how badly he was hurt, but I had to force my worries down., because we still weren't safe yet.

"Come on," Jasin said, taking my elbow.

"Thank you," I told Doran. I had so many mixed feelings about my father, but he'd kept his word and brought me to my mates.

I turned away to follow the others out of the tunnels, but then a cruel voice stopped me in my tracks.

"I should have known you'd betray us, Doran."

7

KIRA

Sark's broad frame filled the tunnel ahead of us, his black armor gleaming under the firelight. His hateful eyes fell on me. "I remember you now. Nysa sent me to find a girl in a small fishing village in the Water Realm and told me to kill her family and bring her back alive. I took care of the parents, but the girl wasn't there. When I went to look for her, Doran stopped me." His cruel gaze snapped back to my father. "You told me she was your daughter, a product of a fling with another woman."

Doran stared the other Dragon down. "Yes, and I said if you told Nysa about her, I'd tell her about your own discretions, and if you touched one hair on Kira's head, I'd kill your granddaughter too. The Fire God's priestess, isn't she?"

My mouth fell open as they argued. Doran had saved my life back then and I'd never known it. Had he been looking out for me all this time without me realizing it? No, I couldn't believe it.

"But you lied," Sark spat. "She's *Nysa's* daughter."

"Yes, but she's still mine." Doran stepped in front of me. "And I won't let you hurt her."

"You fool! We need her. You know that."

"Maybe so, but I can't do this any longer."

"You think any of us want this?" Sark asked. "I've watched my own daughters die too. None of us likes it, but it has to be done."

"Not anymore. It's time this ends. Let her go, and she'll break the cycle. None of our children will have to die again."

Sark stepped forward, his voice menacing. "I can't do that."

Doran sighed. "I had a feeling you'd say that."

His body began to shift and grow, forming scales and wings. "Get Kira out of here," his dragon voice growled, while his large body filled the tunnel. "I'll hold him off and find you later."

Sark had begun to change too, becoming the blood red dragon of my nightmares, while Slade grasped my hand and began to drag me forward.

"No!" I struggled. I'd only just found my father and begun to realize he might not be the monster I'd thought he was. I had too many questions for him, and now they wanted me to leave him behind to fight the man who had haunted my memories for so long. "With all of us here we can take Sark down for good!"

"I know you want to fight him, but this isn't the time," Auric said. "Reven needs you."

I blinked at Auric as his words pierced my red veil of anger. Something about the way he said them made me realize things must be even worse than I'd imagined with Reven. And as much as I wanted to stop Sark, I was exhausted and could barely walk, let alone fight. The others looked weary too from fighting the shades. I sensed dull pain in Jasin as well, which meant he also needed healing. As Auric had said, this wasn't the time for this fight. I reluctantly nodded and began to move forward.

Sark's large red tail slapped down in front of us, blocking our exit and making us jump back. Doran's dragon form wasn't as large but was more agile, and he pounced on top of Sark, knocking him down.

"Go!" he roared, just before Sark rolled back on top and began to tear at my father with his claws.

We took off at a run just as fire began to spew from Sark's mouth and an icy chill permeated the air as Doran fought back. As much as I wanted to stay and help my father, I had a duty to my mates and everyone else. I only prayed I would get a chance to speak with Doran again later.

My mates led me through the dark, musty sewer tunnels, and by the time we emerged we were all drenched and smelling like rotten eggs...or worse. A cart with two horses waited outside, and we climbed into it.

I made sure my mask was securely fastened as Slade urged the horses forward and the cart began to move through the city. I glanced back and saw the tall spires and black arches of the palace, where I'd been held all this time without even knowing it. The main tower rose high in the center, giving Soulspire its name. That was where the Black Dragon was said to live, at the top of that tower. I shuddered at the memory of the last time she came to see me, when I'd learned her true plan.

Jasin wrapped an arm around me. "It's okay. You're free now."

Auric passed me a blanket, which Jasin helped wrap around me.

"The things I learned..." My voice trailed off, and all I could do was shake my head. I had to tell them everything Nysa had said, but the horror was still too great to speak it out loud. In time I would be able to tell them, once we were safe and everyone was healed. But not yet. I was still coming to terms with it myself.

Slade drove the cart through the streets of Soulspire and I gazed about in a daze, taking in the colorful decorations, lively music, and amorous couples. It was hard to believe I'd been trapped in a cage made of bones while all of this joy was going on outside the palace walls. Somewhere in the city Nysa and the other Dragons were making a speech. What would Nysa do when she learned I escaped? Would she hurt Doran?

I leaned my head on Jasin's shoulder, the weariness finally taking its toll. At first, I worried someone would recognize us, but no one cared about a few dirty looking people in a cart, not with the festival going on all around us. Auric grabbed us a few pieces of meat on a stick, which I greedily ate along with some of the apples and oranges in our cart, and then we pulled up at the gate to exit the city. The guards barely even glanced our way as they waved us through. Slade urge the horses forward, and then we were free. I let out a relieved sigh as we left the city behind.

8

KIRA

W e traveled by cart for the rest of the day, worried
we would be spotted if any of my mates shifted
into their Dragon forms. Isen's golden body flew overhead at
one point, but he passed us by without slowing. I watched
the sky for the sight of dark blue wings, but never saw them.
At least I never saw red ones either.

While we traveled into the Earth Realm, the others
filled me in on everything I'd missed while I'd been held
captive. I healed Jasin while snacking on the apples and
oranges in the cart to keep my energy high, then took a long
nap between him and Auric. I avoided questions about what
happened to me during the days I'd been in the bone cage. I
wasn't ready to talk about it yet and would rather wait until
Reven could join us for that conversation anyway.

By the time we stopped to rest for the night, we were all
exhausted. Slade found us a cave that would offer us shelter

44

and protection from the Dragons' eyes, and we spread out inside it and prepared for bed. There was a smaller cave in the back of it, and I followed Slade there once Auric and Jasin had settled down to sleep. I'd noticed that Slade had seemed especially quiet and distant today, and I wanted to make sure he was all right.

I moved behind him and slid my arms around his strong chest, nuzzling my face against the back of his shoulders. "I missed you."

"I missed you too," he said, although his voice was gruffer than normal, and he pulled away from me.

"What's wrong?"

His jaw clenched. "It's my fault you were kidnapped, and my fault that Reven is injured."

"How could that be your fault? The Dragons attacked us, and you defended us the best you could."

He stared at the wall of the cave, which had a thin trickle of water running down it. "Reven stayed behind so I could go after you. He sacrificed himself for us, but I failed to save you. When I went after the Dragons, I couldn't fly. I had to watch them take you away while I stood there, completely useless."

I moved beside him and slowly rubbed his back. "We'd just completed the bond only moments before. No one would expect you to be able to fly so soon. It took Jasin some time before he could fly as well."

"Only a day. And Auric could do it immediately."

"Auric can control wind. He doesn't even need wings to fly. And Jasin was able to practice on our boat with the

45

ELIZABETH BRIGGS

ocean around us in case he fell. You tried to fly off a mountain to rescue me the first time you shifted into your dragon form. That's bravery, not failure."

"I doubt Reven would see it that way."

I grasped his hands with mine. "Reven would understand. If your places were switched, I know you would."

Slade let out a long sigh. "What if I can never fly? I'll be useless to you as a Dragon."

"If Heldor can fly, then surely you can too." I squeezed his hands. "The Earth God picked you for a reason and he believes in you. I believe in you. The others believe in you. Maybe all you need is to believe in yourself." He scowled in response and I pressed a soft kiss to his cheek. "I promise once we heal Reven we'll do whatever it takes to help you fly. You will get there, I'm sure of it."

"I hope you're right." He slid his arms around me and dragged me against his chest, resting his head against mine. "I was so worried I might never see you again, that I'd finally bonded with you only to lose you forever."

"I'm here." I tilted my head to press soft kisses to his neck. "You rescued me. Nothing can keep us apart for long."

His large hands splayed across my back, holding me close. "I want to feel you in my mind the way the others do."

"You will," I promised, and then kissed my way up his neck to his jaw, my lips brushing against his dark beard. "And there is a way to speed it up."

"Is there?"

I slipped my fingers under his shirt, stroking his smooth, muscular stomach. "I've been able to increase the bond with

46

Auric and Jasin by spending time in bed with them. We could get started on that now..."

"Hmm," he said, as his hands slid down to cup my bottom. "We *were* rushed last time, and I promised to make love to you all night long when I could."

"Yes, you did." I pressed against the hard bulge in his trousers and overwhelming need swept through me. I'd been separated from my mates for days, unsure if I would ever see them again, and the only thing I could think about was being close to them now. A primal urge took over, as if the only way to reassure myself Slade was really here with me was to feel him inside me. "And you can have me all night. Just take me now first."

"You're very demanding tonight." He gripped my dark green dress in his hands and dragged it up my legs.

I gave him a coy smile. "Aren't you meant to serve me?"

"And serve you I will." His lips moved to my ear and his deep voice whispered, "Many, many times."

My dress came off and hit the ground, and then Slade's lips were on me, coercing my mouth open. As we kissed, he trailed his fingertips along the underside of my breast, making me arch my back to get closer. His hands were large and rough, the hands of a man who'd spent his life working a forge and a hammer, and I trembled as they moved across my naked skin.

I gripped his shirt and tugged it over his head, desperate to touch him back. The sight of his dark, muscular chest sent a pulsing surge of desire between my thighs. I pressed my palms against his rippling stomach, feeling the coiled strength inside him, before sliding my hands down to undo his trousers. As they fell, he kicked them off of him and stepped back, allowing me to take in the glorious view.

He gestured at the cave wall and the stone moved, forming a short ledge that looked almost like a chair. He sat on it like a king on a throne and beckoned me forward. "Take what you need, my queen."

How could I refuse such an invitation? I climbed onto his lap to straddle him, feeling his rock-hard cock slide against me. My breasts pressed against his muscular chest, my nipples tight with lust, as I lined our bodies up. Slade's green eyes met mine as the anticipation made us both breathe faster, hearts pounding, and then I sank down with one hard push.

He groaned and threw his head back, exposing his thick, dark throat. I kissed the spot right where his beard met his neck and gripped his broad shoulders to steady myself. His hands gripped my waist, and together we began to move as one. I rocked my hips up and down, grinding against the spot where our bodies joined, and he met me with every thrust.

Each roll of my hips pushed his cock even deeper, and the friction of our bodies rubbed me in exactly the right spot to make the pressure build. Slade grabbed my chin and dragged my lips back to his, taking my mouth in a demanding kiss, as his other hand slid to my behind. He squeezed me there, encouraging me to move faster and harder, and I let instinct take over. The bond between us strengthened, allowing us to feel what the other was feeling, and it pushed us both over the edge.

We shattered at the same moment, our bodies so connected it was like one overwhelming orgasm that broke us both apart and then put us back together. Slade crushed me to his chest, claiming my mouth again, as the last tremors of pleasure rumbled through us.

We rocked together for a while, my arms around his neck, our lips dancing across each other's. He held me close in his strong embrace, and I was content to stay in his arms forever.

But after a few minutes Slade lifted me off him, spun me around, and planted me on the ledge—which had now grown into the size of a bed.

"Now it's my turn," Slade said, as he began to move down my body with determined eyes, his mouth finding every spot that made me moan.

I had a feeling neither of us was going to get much sleep that night.

9

REVEN

For a long time, there was nothing but cold, dark pain.

A burst of warmth broke through the chill. A tingling sensation spread through my limbs. Familiar voices echoed through the darkness.

"Not too fast, Jasin," Auric said. "We only want to melt his hands for now."

"Don't worry, I've got this."

That cocky bastard. My lips tried to twitch into a grin but didn't move. Neither did the rest of me. I couldn't speak. I couldn't breathe. I couldn't even open my eyes. What was wrong with me? Where was I?

Soft hands slid into mine, and they felt so hot I would have hissed if I could. "Come back to me, Reven," Kira said, her voice mournful. A wave of relief hit me at the sound, though I wasn't sure why.

"His fingers twitched," Slade said.

"It's working," Auric said. "Start on the rest of him, Jasin. Slowly."

Memories returned in fragments. Kira being kidnapped. Lava striking my side. Heldor bringing down the Earth Temple on my head. And after that only cold, black death.

Except I was still alive.

The chill began to fade and suddenly a burst of air filled my lungs. My heartbeat pounded in my ears. My skin burned and froze at the same time. Agony spread through my limbs and forced my mouth into a scream, though no sound came out. I was alive but starting to wish I wasn't.

Kira's voice was the only thing that held me together, telling me to stay with her over and over. *I'm trying,* I wanted to tell her. I struggled to open my eyes, to get one more glimpse of her, but the pain became too much. I couldn't hold on any longer.

The last thing I heard was the others raising their voices in panic as the darkness took me again.

My eyes snapped open and I jerked to a sitting position, reaching for weapons that weren't there, the memory of pain still fresh in my mind.

"It's okay," Kira said, her arms wrapping around me. "Just relax."

"Kira?" my voice croaked out. I barely recognized it.

"Shh." She stroked my hair with the gentlest touch. "You've been through a lot, but it's over now. I'm here."

My arms wrapped around her and I held her close as I breathed in and out. It took some time before my body stopped trembling and I could let her go. Only then did I realize we were both naked and in bed together. An unfamiliar bed, in an unfamiliar room, but none of that mattered. My gaze traveled down to take her in, and the sight of her lush curves woke me up more than anything. Not that I had the energy to do anything about it at the moment, but I still liked the view.

"How am I alive?" I asked, as I lowered myself back onto the bed. Sitting was too much effort. In fact, everything hurt.

Kira touched my face softly as she settled beside me. "You were badly injured during the fight at the Earth Temple, but you surrounded yourself with ice, which kept you alive in a sort of suspended state. Jasin melted the ice while I healed you."

"I remember." I touched my side and found it healed, though still tender. "How long was I out?"

"Over a week."

"A *week*?" I shook my head, trying to clear it. "The Dragons captured you. Slade stopped them?"

"Not exactly, but I'm safe now. We'll talk about it later. For now, you need to rest and recover. Then we can head to the Water Temple."

Right, the Water Temple. Where we'd be bonded together forever.

I turned on my side to face Kira, grunting with the effort. Emotions churned inside me. Big, scary ones. The kind that made a man want to profess his love for a woman and beg her to stay with him forever. Strong feelings like this made me uncomfortable. So I did the only thing I could. I took her lips in a deep kiss as my hand roamed across her body, cupping her breast and stroking her nipple to make it hard, before moving down her stomach and sliding between her legs. If I turned this to sex, maybe the feelings would release their grip on me.

She gently took my hand to stop me and wove her fingers with mine, then pressed a kiss to my forehead. "Not yet. You need to recover more first. Just let me hold you."

I squeezed my eyes shut, trying to contain the emotions threatening to burst out of me. "It's been a long time since I let anyone hold me."

She wrapped herself around me, her skin sliding against mine. "You can tell yourself it's for healing purposes, if that makes you feel better."

"Is it?" I'd done something similar once when she'd passed out from giving Jasin too much of her strength, and I'd probably used the same damn excuse then too.

"Yes, but it's not the only reason. The guys told me what happened, and then I saw you..." Her voice trembled as her arms squeezed tighter. "I realized how close I'd come to losing you. Now I don't ever want to let you go."

Dammit, those emotions were back and even stronger now. I couldn't keep them in any longer. "Kira, I..."

That was all I got out. I tried to say the words. I wanted to, dammit. But I hadn't said them in so long, and every person I'd said them to had died not long after. I couldn't lose Kira too.

She pressed a soft kiss to my lips. "I know."

I buried my face in her thick red hair, breathing in her scent, and just let her hold me. The turmoil inside me died down, and I relaxed against her. Our naked limbs tangled together, and even though we weren't having sex, it was the most intimate moment of my life. I closed my eyes, and let sleep claim me again.

10

KIRA

Doran arrived a day after Reven woke up. He strolled into the Resistance hideout as if he belonged there, and no one seemed to recognize him in his dusty traveling clothes and heavy cloak. I kept expecting someone to realize he was their enemy, but no one paid him any attention.

At the sight of him walking through Slateden, I was torn between relief and apprehension, unsure if I should run to hug him—or in the opposite direction. The only thing I could think to say was, "You're alive."

He smirked and tipped his head. "Sark and I can't kill each other, though Gods know we've tried many times over the years. The bond with Nysa prevents us from doing anything other than roughing each other up a bit. But don't worry, I made sure he couldn't follow me here."

"Thank you for helping us. I'm not sure I could have escaped without you."

"Of course. Unfortunately, Nysa and her mates all know I've betrayed them by now. I can't go back to Soulspire." He chuckled as he pushed back his hood. "Guess that means I'll be sticking with you for the rest of your journey. Now, where can I get some food around here? I'm starving."

Sticking with us? I wasn't sure how I felt about it, but I had more pressing things I wanted to talk about first. "I can have something brought up for us. I have a lot of questions for you."

"I'm sure you do, and I'll do my best to answer them all. While we eat."

I gathered all my mates and my father into a room that Parin had once used to meet with spies and soldiers. Now that he was gone and Faya was busy trying to keep the Resistance running, the room had sat unused. Food and drinks were placed along the long wooden table, and although I'd asked for something simple, the kitchen staff had outdone themselves. I suspected many people in Slateden were feeling aimless without their leader and needed something to channel their energy into.

My mates sat around the table and none of them looked happy to be there. Jasin glared at Doran while loading a plate with food. Slade leaned back and crossed his arms, his face stony. Auric spread his journal and quill out on the table and prepared to take notes. Reven sat beside me and watched Doran closely, but his face was paler than normal. This morning I'd told them all about my time being held captive by the Dragons, and about how Nysa had stayed alive so long, and they weren't particularly pleased with Doran right now.

Doran began shoveling food into his mouth, ignoring the suspicious looks the others gave him. I watched him for a long moment, studying his face, still shocked to be sitting across from my true father. My father, who had done nothing to stop Nysa for years.

"Is it true?" I asked, my throat tightening. "All those children before me?"

His face turned grim and he set down his fork. "It's true. Every thirty years Nysa bears a daughter, who should become the next Spirit Dragon if the cycle was allowed to continue. Except Nysa drains their life and their inherent magic to keep herself alive, along with the rest of us."

"And you just let that happen?" Jasin asked.

"For a long time, yes. It's not something I'm proud of, but for many years I thought it was necessary. It was only when Kira was born that I realized how corrupted Nysa had become, and how she'd tainted the rest of us through our bond with her."

"Why was I any different?" I asked. "And how did I survive?"

Doran's eyes met mine. "You survived because, for the first time in all our years, Nysa had twins."

His words slammed into my chest, knocking me off balance. At first I couldn't speak, too stunned, trying to make sense of what he'd said. Finally I whispered, "I have a sister?"

"You did," Doran said, his face darkening with pain. "It

had been many years since I'd sired a child with Nysa. All of us traded off to ease the burden of watching our own children be sacrificed, but it was eventually my turn again. I wanted to stop Nysa, but the bond makes it difficult for us to act against her, and we'd all resigned ourselves to the fact that we could do nothing." He drew in a long breath before continuing. "When I learned Nysa was having twins, I realized I had a chance to save one of them. Your sister was born first, and Nysa drained her immediately. She never even got a name, as most of them didn't, but I called her Sora, after my mother. While Nysa was busy with her, I named you Kira, after my sister, and switched you with a baby who had died only hours before during childbirth. A servant rushed you out of the palace and to safety, while I informed Nysa that her second child hadn't made it."

Tears welled up in my eyes at the thought of the twin sister I'd never known, and anger filled me knowing Nysa had killed her and Doran had done nothing to stop her. "Why didn't you save both of us?"

"I wanted to, more than anything, but it wasn't possible. Nysa needed a sacrifice to keep herself alive. If I had taken both of you, Nysa would have scoured the earth until the two of you were found. She wouldn't have stopped until you were both drained, making her doubly powerful." He stared at the plate in front of him, his voice low. "Your sister's sacrifice allowed you to live. If I could have done it any other way I would have, and I've spent the last twenty years trying to make sure Nysa never found out you were alive, so that your sister's death wasn't in vain. But I still mourn Sora every day, along with all the other daughters I've lost over the centuries."

Slade reached over and took my hand under the table, and Auric did the same on the other side. I gripped their hands hard, fighting back tears as heaviness filled my chest. *Sora*, my soul called out, searching for this missing part of myself. I hadn't known she'd existed before this day, but there had always been an emptiness inside me I'd never understood. Maybe all those years I'd spent running, searching for a family, and longing for someone to love me was my way of trying to find my lost twin again. But I wasn't sure there was anything that could fill that void.

I pushed my plate away, my appetite gone. My mates stared at me, and I felt their sympathetic worry through the bond. There was nothing they could do to help with this though. It had been bad enough knowing Nysa had killed my sisters for hundreds of years, but learning she'd taken my twin too...

By the Gods, I was going to make her pay.

I wanted to rush back to Soulspire and take her out this instant, but I couldn't let anger drive me into doing something foolish. I had to learn more before I could do anything, and I still had a lot of questions for my father.

I drew in a deep breath to steady myself and focused on one of the other questions. "The people who raised me... who were they?"

"Your mother was my great-granddaughter, the result of an affair I had long ago. She was the last of my descendants, and she took you in and swore to protect you." Doran's fist clenched around a biscuit, turning it to crumbs. "I'll never forgive Sark for what he did to her."

That explained why we looked so similar, except for our hair color. My adopted mother's hair was long and blond, which I realized now was the same shade as Doran's hair.

Doran wiped his hands on a napkin. "I've watched you from the shadows your entire life, Kira. I've tried not to interfere too much, but I've always been there, working to keep you safe. Unfortunately, that often meant acting as Nysa's devoted servant for much of your life. It's freeing to know I don't have to continue that act any longer."

Auric paused from scribbling in his journal and looked up. "What about your bond with Nysa? Won't she be able to find you here?"

Doran shook his head. "Over the years I learned how to block Nysa through the bond. It helps that I haven't slept with her since before Kira was born either. The bond between us has naturally weakened over time." He ran a rough hand over his scraggly beard, his eyes distant. "It's hard because I still love her, despite everything she's done. I always will. But she's become...corrupted. And through the bond, the rest of us became corrupted too. I was able to find my way out of it, but the others are too far gone. Which is why they all need to be defeated."

"You want us to kill your mate," Reven said, his eyes narrowed.

"It's the only way to stop her and to save Kira." Doran pushed his seat back as if he was about to stand. "There's a lot more I need to tell you, which will help you understand

Nysa better and how she became so corrupted, but we need to start heading toward the Water Temple as soon as possible. Only once you've bonded with all four of your mates can you hope to stand against her."

"But the Water Temple was destroyed," Slade said.

"And the Dragons know we'll be going there," Jasin added. "They'll be waiting for us."

"No, they won't," Doran said. "And it hasn't been destroyed, because I moved it years ago. None of the Dragons know where the real Water Temple is. I made sure of that."

"Where is it?" Auric asked, his quill clenched in his hand and his eyes bright with the promise of secret knowledge.

"In the far reaches of the Water Realm. It will take us a few days to get there, so I suggest we leave as soon as we're able to."

"It depends on Reven," I said, glancing at him. "He's still recovering and—"

"I'm fine," he said quickly. "I'm ready to go."

Doran stood and glanced around the table. "Then I guess it's time for us to head out."

11

KIRA

That evening there was a small funeral for Parin, now that most people had returned from the battle at Salt Creek Tower. As the ceremony began, Slade opened up a large hole in the side of the mountain with a mighty tremble that seemed to shake the entire world. Parin's body had been cleaned and prepared, and members of the Resistance lowered it into the hole while Faya watched with stoic eyes. Once Parin was placed inside, Faya dropped in the small jade carving of a dragon, meant to represent the Earth God, which Parin's mother had made. Slade then covered up the tomb with dirt and rocks, allowing Parin to become one with the mountain that housed the Resistance hideout. As the son of the Earth God's High Priestess, it seemed a fitting resting place for him.

When it was over, there was a somber celebration with food and soft music in Faya's house. I wanted to offer my condolences to her and to tell her that Parin was a hero, but she was surrounded at all times by other people. I even saw my father speak to her for a few minutes, and I wondered who Faya thought he was. A strange traveler come to join their cause? Just another member of the Resistance?

"Kira," Brin said, drawing my attention away from my father. She threw her arms around me and gave me a quick squeeze. "I'm so glad you're okay. When the others told me what happened I was worried, although I knew you'd find a way out."

"I only escaped thanks to my mates and..." My eyes found my father again.

She followed my gaze. "Who is that? I saw him with you earlier."

I wanted to tell her. In fact, I was desperate to talk to her and have some girl time, but not here. Too many people surrounded us, and I didn't want them to hear what I had to say. "Would Leni mind if I dragged you off to talk?"

Brin glanced over at her girlfriend, who was speaking with Slade. "I doubt it. Besides, a little jealousy now and then only spices things up, right?"

We walked out of the house, although not before Brin grabbed a bottle of wine and some tiny little cakes and pastries. Once back in my guest room we eagerly kicked off our shoes and climbed onto the bed, sitting across from each other. A pang of sadness shot through me at the memory of doing this with my best friend, Tash, and the reminder that I never would again. Sark had taken that from me, like he'd taken so many other things.

Brin poured us some wine before spreading the desserts out in front of us. She eyed them carefully, before plucking a flaky pastry from the plate. "All right, I'm ready."

I chugged a big gulp of wine. "The man you saw...he's my father."

Her eyes widened. "Really? Wait. Does that mean...?"

"Yes, he's a Dragon. The Azure one."

"Wow. I've never met him before, only Sark and Isen. What's he doing here?"

"He's left the Black Dragon and has joined our cause. He wants to protect me and help me defeat her. Or so he says."

She took a bite of her pastry as she considered this. "What's he like?"

I picked up my own pastry and eyed it. "I'm not sure yet. He helped me escape and he's given me some answers about my past, but it's hard to trust him, knowing what he is. Even if I do learn to trust him and get to know him, it's my destiny to overthrow him." My throat grew tight. "To defeat the Black Dragon, I have to kill all her mates first. That includes my father."

Her eyes turned sympathetic. "What are you going to do?"

"I don't know yet." I took a bite of my pastry, sending flaky bits all over the bed. "There's more too. When I was being held captive, I met my mother. She was beautiful, regal, and...she's a monster."

I quickly told Brin everything that had happened and what I'd learned about my sisters, including my twin. Brin let me get it all out, and it was so good to talk to someone who wasn't directly involved, like my mates were. They all wanted to leap over themselves to protect me, shelter me, and make me happy, but Brin could just listen and offer unbiased advice. Sometimes that's all I needed.

"This definitely calls for more wine." Brin poured more wine into my glass from the bottle she'd swiped. "Eat another dessert too, it'll make you feel better."

"What do you think I should do?" I asked, before shoving a bite-size raspberry cake into my mouth.

Brin tapped her nails against the glass while I chewed. "I think you should listen to Doran and ask him more questions. He obviously has a great deal of information, and he's probably your best bet for learning how to actually defeat the other Dragons, but keep your distance too. Even if everything he says is true, he's not innocent in all of this. He's part of the reason Nysa is in power and the world is in chaos."

I nodded. "We need him to get to the Water Temple. I'll try to learn more on our journey."

"And when the time comes to defeat the Dragons?"

I stared into my wine. "I'll do what I have to do, I suppose."

Brin leaned forward and gave me a squeeze. "You're strong. You can do this."

"Thanks. There are some days—okay, a lot of days lately —when it all seems overwhelming and impossible."

"Just take it day by day, step by step. Like crossing things off a list. Step one: get to the Water Temple and bond with that sexy assassin of yours." She nudged me with her elbow. "At least you'll get some action from Reven finally."

I couldn't help but smile at that. Trust Brin to find the bright side if it involved sex. "I am looking forward to that part."

"I don't blame you. If I liked men, I'd be drooling over him too."

"How are you and Leni doing, anyway?"

Her face lit up at the mention of her girlfriend. "We're good. Really good. From the moment we met I felt this spark, but sometimes that goes away quickly. The spark with Leni hasn't burnt out yet." She leaned back and smiled, her face relaxed. "Now that I don't have marriage to Auric hanging over my head, I'm truly free to be who I want to be, and I can be with the person I want to be with."

"I'm happy for you. I really like Leni." I swirled my wine in my glass. "What are you going to do now? Do you want to come with us to the Water Temple?"

"I do, but I think I should stay here. The Resistance lost a lot of people at the Salt Creek Tower battle and Parin is gone. Leni and I can do some good here if we stay. For once, I feel like I've found somewhere I can be more than just a rich noble, attending parties and flirting with dignitaries. I can do some good here. Make a difference." Her voice had turned serious and now she shook it off with a grin. "Besides, you don't really need me. You have your four muscular mates and the Azure Dragon too."

"I always need you as my friend, but the Resistance is lucky to have your help."

She sat up a bit. "I actually have a specific idea for something I wanted to run past you."

My eyebrows shot up. "What is it?"

"Rumors are beginning to spread about you and your mates. I'd like to encourage them."

"Why?"

"It gives people something to fight for, and it'll spread hope. The world is ready for a change in leadership, and people have been oppressed for too long. New Dragons rising up to challenge the old ones? The Resistance would be overflowing with new recruits."

I brushed crumbs off myself and the bed. "I see your point. Do whatever you think is best. We're not hiding anymore, and you're right that it's time the world knows about us."

"Exactly. Although we need to call you all something else. We can't have two Crimson Dragons, and so forth. That's just way too confusing for the general public."

I hadn't thought of that before, but Enva had mentioned she'd been called the White Dragon, so it seemed the names were changeable. "You can call us the ascendants. That's what the priests and Gods say."

"That works, but I think we need something more too." She tapped her lips in thought. "What if we use gemstones? We can call Jasin the Ruby Dragon, for example. It'll distance him from the Crimson Dragon's reputation, which would be a good thing. Crimson makes one think of all the blood Sark has spilled. Rubies are regal, beautiful, and passionate. Then we can use emerald, citrine, and sapphire for the other men."

"I like it, but not sure the men will. And what will they call me?"

"The White Dragon? It has a nice contrast to the Black Dragon."

"No, that's what my grandmother was called. How about the Silver Dragon?"

"Perfect." She clinked her glass against mine. "Trust me. This is what I'm good at, and with the support of the people, you'll have a much easier time rallying people to your cause, and maintaining order once you defeat the Dragons."

"I hope it goes that smoothly." Great, something else to worry about. I'd spent so much time trying to figure out how to defeat the Dragons I hadn't stopped to consider what would happen if we won. All I knew was that I didn't want to rule, not like my mother. I just wanted peace.

"It will all work out," Brin reassured me. "Just promise me you'll come back after the Water temple and fill me in on everything."

"I will. I'll probably need someone to talk to after dealing with my four mates plus my father." I groaned at the thought. "I think this is going to be a long journey."

12

KIRA

We left for the Water Realm in the morning, beginning a journey that would take many days and return me to the place where I'd grown up. I'd avoided going back ever since I'd left when I was thirteen, and I both longed to see the sparkling blue waters again and dreaded returning to the place where I'd lost my family. I wondered if Reven felt the same. Our childhoods had so many similarities, at least from the bits and pieces I'd learned from him, and I wished he would open up to me more, but it was something I couldn't force.

He was doing better physically, at least. Some color had returned to his face, and he no longer looked quite as frail and thin. I tried to touch him as much as possible, hoping my healing would help him recover faster, and to reassure myself he was truly all right.

We soared southwest across the Earth Realm, leaving

behind the ice-covered mountain peaks and flying over forests and fields. There'd been some argument over which dragon I would ride, with everyone saying that Doran couldn't be trusted. Both Jasin and Auric wanted me to fly with them, but that meant Slade or Reven would have to ride with my father. In the end, I decided to have faith in Doran and told my mates I'd be riding with him—end of discussion. They didn't like it, but Doran had proven himself so far, and I wanted to show I trusted him, even if I was still hesitant about it. I hoped it might bring us closer, and as a result of that he might reveal more about the past.

And maybe I just wanted to be near my father too. I'd spent my entire life yearning and searching for a family. I'd moved from place to place, trying to find a replacement for the parents I'd lost and the twin sister I never knew I was missing. First I'd tried to find my family with merchants, then with bandits, before landing with Tash and her mother. Now my family consisted of my mates, but I loved them in a different way.

A part of me knew that my relationship with my father would be fleeting and short-lived. I wanted to soak up as much time with him as I could before it was over. Even if he was something of a monster, I was curious about him—and my mother too, if I was honest. They'd lived a long time, and I knew so little about them, beyond the myths and rumors.

"What did you do before you became Nysa's mate?" I asked, when we stopped to take a quick break. Talking while flying was difficult except for a few short words yelled into the wind, so this was our first moment to chat.

"I was a pirate," Doran said.

"Really?" I had to admit he did look the part.

He leaned against a tree and took a swig of water. "It's been a long time since I thought about those days. I grew up in the Water Realm, and your grandmother and her mates had brokered a truce with the elementals, so they didn't attack us as long as we stayed out of their way. That opened the seas to travel, and I joined a merchant's ship at thirteen. At sixteen, we got attacked by pirates. They told me I could join them or die. Seemed like an obvious choice." A slow grin spread over his face. "By the time I was twenty-five and the Water God came to visit me, I was captain of that ship."

"What happened then?"

His grin faded. "I gave it all up for Nysa."

Of course he did. Just like my mates gave up their previous lives for me. "Did you love her?"

"I did. I do. I always will." He met my eyes. "But I love my daughter more."

I stared at him and grasped for a way to respond. He turned away before I could find an answer, and then he shifted back into his dragon form to take off. All I could do was stand there, reeling in shock, while a warm feeling spread through my chest, followed by a deep, unbearable sadness. I'd waited so long to hear words like that...and now they were from my enemy.

D oran led the way, pushing us hard the entire time. When we finally stopped it was late in the evening, and we managed to find an abandoned farm to spend the night in. The roof was caving in on the farmhouse and everything had a layer of dust, but I supposed it was better than camping outside. Jasin lit a fire in the slightly moldy hearth, and we sat around it while we ate some of the food we'd packed.

Doran spread the map out in front of us. "We're going to take a slightly longer route to avoid the other Dragons, who will no doubt be looking for us around the old Water Temple."

"What can you tell us about the other Dragons?" Jasin asked.

He lifted one shoulder in a casual shrug. "What do you want to know? I've spent many lifetimes with the bastards. It's hard to narrow it down to a quick summary."

"Tell us about each one of them," Auric said. "What did they do before they were chosen by the Gods? What are they like now?"

Doran leaned back in a rickety wooden chair and folded his hands behind his head. "Isen was a nobleman, Sark was a soldier, Heldor was a carpenter, and, like I told Kira earlier, I was a pirate."

"That sounds oddly similar to our lives before all of this," Slade said.

"You're probably more like the Dragon you're replacing than you realize, and you'll probably take on similar roles once this is all over. Her protector, her enforcer, her scout, and her diplomat." He chuckled softly. "What can I say? Each of the Gods has a type."

"I'm nothing like Sark," Jasin said with a scowl.

"No? He's brave, passionate, and hot-tempered. He acts without thinking but can be strategic when it comes to battle. He'd fight and die for his beliefs and he's willing to stand up and be a leader when required. Sound like anyone we know?" He smirked, and Jasin's scowl only deepened. "But you're right—Sark is different from you in some ways. He will murder innocents, including children, and feels no guilt as long as he believes it will help the Black Dragon. Sark's the darker version of you, twisted and corrupted by years of serving Nysa."

"Does that make you the darker version of me?" Reven asked, arching an eyebrow.

"I suppose." Doran appraised Reven. "We both have a view of the world that's more gray than black and white. We're both willing to do whatever needs to be done, preferably from the shadows. We collect secrets to use as leverage. We guard our hearts and can come across as cold, but only to hide how much we feel. Am I right?"

Reven looked away sharply and didn't answer.

I leaned forward, curious. "What makes you darker than him?"

Doran's face turned serious. "I doubt Reven would have waited centuries to act when he believed something was wrong."

Awkward silence fell over the room. "And Heldor?" I finally asked.

"Heldor is fiercely loyal to the Black Dragon and rarely leaves her side unless she commands it. Most of us have had other lovers over the years, but Heldor has never once strayed. He's the strong and silent type, calm under pressure, and generally level-headed. But he has a low tolerance for nonsense, and he follows Nysa without question. He'll do anything for her."

"What about Isen?" Auric asked.

"Isen is smart, calculating, and likes to collect knowledge, although his motives are different from yours. For him, it's all about power. In the old days, he was often the mediator of our group, and trust me there were many times when none of us got along. He prefers not to fight unless he must, although he has no problem murdering people in cold blood either. His favorite method is to suffocate anyone who disagrees with him." Doran turned to Auric. "I can teach you how to do that, if you'd like."

"No, thank you." Auric's face paled. "That sounds horrible."

"Why hasn't Isen done that to us?" Jasin asked.

"Suffocating someone with magic requires a lot of concentration, and it takes longer than you think to choke someone to death. He prefers to use it to make sure he gets his way—anyone watching is usually too terrified to disagree with him after that."

"How do we defeat them?" Slade asked.

Doran let out a harsh laugh. "Right now? You can't.

They're stronger than you, and they've been Dragons for centuries."

Reven sneered. "What are we supposed to do? Wait a hundred years before trying to take them down?"

"No, because I'm going to train you." My father leaned forward, the firelight dancing in his eyes. "I'll teach you how to use your powers and how to work together. In our time, the previous Dragons mentored us before they stepped down. You've been at a disadvantage because you've had to figure everything out on your own." He looked at each of us in turn. "With my help, you might actually stand a chance."

13

SLADE

In the morning, I woke early and took a walk through the abandoned farm, down a steep hill. When I was out of sight of the farmhouse, I shifted into my dragon form for the second time. The transformation was strange as my bones cracked, expanded, and changed. Wings formed on my back. My fingernails turned to talons. My teeth turned to fangs. And everything around me suddenly got a lot smaller.

Compared to the others, I was massive. In my human form I was broader than Kira's other mates, but I hadn't realized it would translate to this body as well.

I glanced behind me again to make sure no one had followed me, trying to get used to the way my long neck moved, almost like a snake's. With the sun cresting the horizon, my scales turned to green fire, and I had to admit they were beautiful.

I took a deep breath and raised my wings. The fear of

failing a second time nearly held me back, but I had to try this again. For Kira.

I beat my wings as fast as I could and managed to lift up onto my claws, but that was as far as I got. It was like the ground itself was holding me down, preventing me from flying. I let out a frustrated roar before becoming a human again.

I knelt and picked up a handful of dirt, then let it run through my fingers. Would I ever be able to fly, or would I be condemned to the ground forever?

"Heldor had difficulty flying at first, too," Doran said, making me jump. He stood behind me, appearing out of nowhere like Reven did sometimes. Sneaky bastards. "It's not your fault. Your Earth magic makes it hard for you to fly. That connection with the ground is so strong you'll have to learn to overcome and let go of it before you can lift off. I can help you." He examined me. "It doesn't help you're such a large Dragon either, about the same size as Heldor when you shift. You'll need to build up your wing strength too."

I scowled at him, but his words felt right, and I had to admit I did need help. I had no idea what I was doing, and I didn't have time to figure it out on my own. He'd lived for hundreds of years and had seen Heldor go through the same thing once. I gritted my teeth and said, "I'd appreciate your help."

Doran chuckled. "I doubt that, but I'll give it to you anyway. There's no way you can defeat us if you can't fly."

"You *want* us to defeat you?"

"Of course." He said it casually, so casually I suspected

he might be lying. Like Reven, he was hard to read, and secrets perpetually danced behind his eyes. Until recently, I wouldn't have trusted either of them. Then Reven went and saved my life and nearly died in the process. And Doran... Well, he'd helped Kira escape and had protected her. I wasn't ready to let down my guard completely with him, but I was willing to listen to his advice.

Doran waved a hand at me. "All right, turn back into a dragon."

"You want to do this now?"

"You have somewhere else you need to be?"

I scowled at him, then took a few steps back to give myself space, and returned to my dragon form. The others would be up soon, but for now we were alone out here.

He nodded as if confirming his suspicions. "Like I thought, your size is going to make it harder for you to fly. You'll need to practice with your wings every day to build up their strength."

I groaned, though it came out more like a growl. My voice was different as a dragon. Deeper. Louder. More gravely.

"But the real thing holding you back is your own magic," Doran continued. "Along with your own self-doubt."

Now I really did growl at him, though he ignored it and kept talking.

"What I want you to do is try to let go of your earth magic. I know it's a part of you but try to block it out however you can."

How did he expect me to do that? The moment the

Earth God came to me, I became a different person. No longer a simple blacksmith living in a small town, but someone destined for bigger things. Even when I wondered if he should have chosen another, or missed my old life, or tried to guard my heart from Kira, I'd never wavered in my faith. The magic was a fundamental part of me and had become as natural as breathing.

I felt the earth through my clawed feet, which dug at the dirt. The only time I didn't feel the earth's presence was when I was flying on one of the other dragons' backs, or when we were on a wretched boat. Even on a boat I'd managed to connect with the wood and the metal, but soaring high in the sky—it was hard for me to feel comfortable with that. Like a part of me was cut off.

Maybe that was the problem. I tried to focus on that uncomfortable feeling now. I pictured riding on the back of Auric or Jasin as they soared across the sky, and how empty and adrift I felt. I hated it, but when I tried to take off this time, my feet left the ground.

I didn't get far. My wings flapped rapidly to hold me up, but I knew they wouldn't last long.

From below, Doran called out, "Nice work! Try to hold it as long as you can."

I hovered above him for a few more seconds, before hitting the ground in a thump, sending a cloud of dirt into the air around us.

Doran coughed and waved it away. "Good. Now I want you to do that every day. Preferably multiple times."

I groaned and set my head down, already tired from that short flight—and from dealing with Doran.

He walked away while I rested there, enjoying the sun on my back and the dirt under my scales. As the sky grew brighter, I heard footsteps approach. Kira. I raised my head and met her eyes before looking away quickly, ashamed she had to see me like this. I was a failed dragon who could hover for a few seconds at best. She deserved better.

"I never got the chance to see you as a dragon," she said, as she approached. Her arms wrapped around my head, embracing me. "You're beautiful."

I let out a grunt, but nudged my head up against her chest, enjoying her touch. The bond between us, which I hadn't noticed before except when we'd had sex, suddenly took over my mind. I sensed how happy she was to see me like this and felt her belief in me. My own doubts slowly fell away. I couldn't fly now, but I would keep practicing every spare moment I could—for Kira.

14

KIRA

We reached the coast that evening, just north of the border between the Earth Realm and the Water Realm. Doran showed Reven and Slade how to turn saltwater into water we could drink, while Auric and Jasin rested after flying the entire day with few breaks. I took a walk down the shore, my toes digging into the wet sand for the first time in years, while lazy waves stretched closer and closer to my feet. The moon was bright overhead, making the surface of the water shimmer, and I bent to pick up a shell that almost seemed to glow.

"Kira," a voice whispered across the salty breeze.

I jerked upright and spun around, the shell clutched in my palm. My grandmother Enva stood ankle-deep in the water, yet when the tide pulled back, she showed no signs it had ever touched her. She strode toward me, her gray skirts completely dry, her white hair shining under the moonlight like a pearl. She'd once been called the White Dragon, and though she'd been dead for centuries, she was trapped between this world and the next along with every other person who had passed. But unlike the others, her connection to the Spirit Goddess allowed her to hold onto enough life to manifest in front of me for a short time.

"I'm sorry I couldn't help while you were being held captive," she said, as she drew near. "The bone cage prevented me from visiting you."

"I assumed as much," I said, relieved to see her again. "Why does the bone block our powers?"

"Your magic stems from life, and bones are objects of death. They're abhorrent to us, completely opposite of our very nature."

I frowned as I examined the shell in my palm. "But I've killed many animals and even people before. I've been around many dead bodies. It wasn't until I touched Tash's bones that I encountered that horrible feeling."

"Ah, because there's a difference between killing to preserve life, and killing only to end it. When you hunt animals for food for yourself or others, you're sustaining life. When you've killed people, it was to defend yourself or protect other lives. All of those things are part of the natural cycle of survival. But when someone is murdered, their bones become tainted with darkness."

"Nysa could touch them. How?"

Enva's face darkened. "That is the ultimate question. I suggest you ask your father."

I stared at her, while wind tugged on my hair and completely ignored hers. "So Doran truly is my father."

"Of course. But you knew that already."

"I did, but I wanted to hear you confirm it. Why didn't you tell me?"

"It wasn't my place, and I knew you wouldn't take it well. Not at that time."

I sighed. She was probably right. "What of everything he told me about Nysa—is it all true?"

"Yes, he has been honest with you. He's just left out something very important. Something you should ask him about."

"What is that?"

Enva's eyes burned into mine. For the first time I realized they were the same green as my mother's. "Nysa told you she has to stay alive in order to keep the Spirit Goddess contained. Ask him why."

I nodded slowly. "I assumed it was so the Gods couldn't replace her."

"Not entirely. I would tell you myself, but it's a long tale and I expect you'll have many questions. I already feel the other side pulling me back now."

"I wish we had more time together. There's so much I want to know about your life. Like what was it like when you were a Dragon? Doran said you negotiated a treaty with the elementals and brought peace?"

"Every set of Dragons has one great challenge to face. Mine was the elementals. When I became the White Dragon, the elementals had ravaged the four Realms and humans were living in fear. The balance had tipped too far in one direction, and my mates and I did what we could to level the scales again." She gazed across the water with a distant look in her eyes. "For some time, we had peace. And then the shades came."

"Was that my mother's challenge?" I asked.

"It was the start of it." Enva sighed and stared at the sand at her feet. "There's another reason Doran should tell you this tale. It hurts me too much to speak it aloud. I love my daughter, no matter how twisted she's become. I understand why she did what she did, even if I disagreed with it. I only wish I could have prevented all of this or found a way to save her from the darkness. I'm her mother, and I failed her...and now I must help you defeat her."

I took her hand, which felt solid even though she wasn't really there. "No one should have to make such a choice."

She squeezed my hand in return as she began to fade before my eyes. "Nysa and I both made mistakes, but I know you will be the one to right them. Stay strong, Kira..."

She disappeared from sight as her last words floated away on the wind. A sense of sadness filled me as I stood alone with the waves lapping at my bare feet while I clutched a shell in my hand. I released it into the water and turned to walk the distance back to my mates, while I mentally prepared myself for another conversation with my father. One that I wasn't sure I was ready to have.

I stepped through the camp the others had set up, past a bonfire Jasin had started, where fresh fish now roasted. My mates stirred as I strode past them but must have seen the serious expression on my face because none of them said a word. Doran was stretched out in front of the ocean, leaning back as he gazed up at the stars, his hands folded across his stomach. He looked up as I approached and his expression changed, as if he sensed that something had occurred, but he wasn't sure exactly what.

I stopped in front of him and met his eyes. "Tell me about the Spirit Goddess."

15

KIRA

My father ran a hand over his beard, which was looking more rugged with each day that went by. "I'd planned to tell you about this once we reached the Water Temple, but I suppose now is as good a time as any. Sit down. This might take a while. And someone get me some ale."

I sank onto the ground across from him, pulling my knees to my chest, while my mates gathered around. "Nysa told me she had to drain my life in order to contain the Spirit Goddess. What does that mean? Why would she need to contain her?"

Doran scrounged up a bottle of something dark from his pack and popped off the top of it. "I'll get to that, but I need to start at the beginning. The first thing you need to know is that the Spirit Goddess is really two entities: Life and

Death. Twin sisters, two sides of the same coin, bound together as one."

Auric grabbed his notebook and began furiously scribbling in it. "Why have we never heard of this before?"

"All records of this are long gone. Nysa made sure of that." My father took a long swig of his alcohol before continuing. "Long before any of us were on this earth, the Spirit Goddess ruled with her four mates, the other Gods of Fire, Earth, Air, and Water. They created the elementals to represent each God and humans to represent the Goddess. But over the years the Death side of her became too strong and corrupted the Spirit Goddess. The balance of life and death shifted too far to one side. To stop the world from falling into darkness, the Gods broke up the two aspects of Life and Death, creating two separate Goddesses instead of one. The Death Goddess was banished to the Realm of the Dead, where she became its ruler, while the Life Goddess stayed here with her four mates. They created the Dragons to act as their representatives in the world, and to make sure that the Death Goddess could never return."

"I thought the Dragons were created to keep the balance between elementals and humans," Jasin said.

"That is one of their duties, yes. But they were also created to ensure that the Life Goddess had assistance in protecting the world from the Death Goddess. Kira you are actually a descendant of the Life Goddess, as were all the other female Dragons before you."

That would explain why the bone cage harmed me the

way it did, but not why my mother was immune to it. "What about Nysa?"

"I'm getting to that." Doran scowled and stared at his bottle. "When Nysa turned twenty, she became a Dragon, like her mother. Back then she wasn't dark or evil, not like you know her now."

"What happened?" Slade asked.

He took another chug of his drink as he gazed into the fire. "Shortly after she became a Dragon, shades began appearing in our world in vast numbers, sucking the life from both elementals and humans alike. We learned later that they were the creation of the Death Goddess. She'd grown tired of living in the Realm of the Dead and jealous of her twin for having all four mates to herself. She sent the shades to attack us, and they fed her power with each life they took. Soon, she had enough power to leave the afterlife and return to our world. When she did, she brought death and darkness everywhere she went, and every time she took a life, she grew stronger. And with the Death Goddess gone, the way to the Realm of the Dead closed, trapping all fallen souls between the two worlds. No one has been able to find peace since then."

"Enva mentioned that," I said, nodding.

Doran arched an eyebrow. "How do you know of her?"

"She comes to visit me sometimes."

"Does she? Interesting." His eyes turned haunted, the firelight flickering in his eyes. "Yes, the Death Goddess's arrival changed everything. The Life Goddess fought her twin sister, but their battle nearly tore the entire world apart. The Death Goddess had become too powerful from all the lives she had stolen. As a last resort, we worked with the Gods to bind the two Goddesses together again, but all it did was create a dark, twisted Spirit Goddess who began to devour all life with an insatiable hunger. We realized we'd made a terrible mistake, but the other Gods refused to help us separate them again. The Spirit Goddess was their mate, their queen, their leader, and they had to obey her. So we decided all the Gods had to be stopped, for the sake of the world."

"How do you stop a God?" Reven asked.

"It's not easy." Doran drained the last of his bottle and tossed it aside. "We imprisoned all the Gods in their temples, one by one, using the element that is their opposite. Fire versus water, earth versus air, you get the idea. Once they were gone the Spirit Goddess was weakened and we tried to imprison her in the Spirit Temple, but we failed. She was too strong, even then. But Nysa found a way to cage the Spirit Goddess...by trapping her within her own body."

I gasped. "The Spirit Goddess is *inside* Nysa?"

"She is. It was the only way to stop her, although we didn't realize the consequences of doing such a thing." His jaw clenched. "Nysa fought against the Death Goddess's darkness for years, but eventually she succumbed to it and became the Black Dragon. She still maintains some control, which is how she keeps the Spirit Goddess contained, but she's become twisted...and incredibly powerful. She controls both life and death magic, along with all the elements, making her nearly unstoppable. With a single touch, she can drain a person's life, and her body heals itself immediately. That's on the rare occasions she is injured at all, since she's immune to all five elements."

I dug my toes into the sand, taking in everything he'd said. It was a lot to absorb, and it made our task seem even more daunting. "Is it even possible to defeat Nysa? And if we do, what will happen?"

"It's possible but won't be easy. And if Nysa dies, the Spirit Goddess will be unleashed upon the world again. This is why she started sacrificing her own children...and why we reluctantly went along with it."

"I don't see how any of you could agree to that," Slade said with disgust, echoing my own thoughts.

"No, because you didn't see how bad it was when the Spirit Goddess was free. She would have wiped out all life on this world within months. If we let her continue, this would be a second Realm of the Dead under her rule." Doran pinched the bridge of his nose. "Nysa was desperate to keep the Spirit Goddess contained, and she tried draining humans, elementals, and shades, but none of it extended her life. But then she had a daughter, continuing the Dragon cycle. The magic within the child was strong enough to keep Nysa—and by extension the rest of us—alive for another thirty years, when she could have another child." He shuddered a little. "It was horrible, but we told ourselves it was one life taken in exchange for millions saved. We didn't realize what the toll would be on our own souls."

"And yet you kept doing it," Jasin growled. "For hundreds of years."

My father dropped his head. "We had no other choice. Until Kira and her twin sister were born."

"Why were we different?" I asked.

Doran's eyes rested on me again. "All of our daughters were born with both life and death magic inside them, except for the two of you. Your magic was split, with Kira having life magic, and Sora having death magic. I thought it was a sign that the Spirit Goddess could be divided again, and our mistakes could finally be undone." He clenched his fists in the sand. "After I got Kira to safety, I released the Fire God from his prison. I was the only one who could do it, since I'd been the one who put him there. Once the Fire God was freed, he helped me release the other Gods one by one in secret, so that they could choose Dragons for Kira's mates when her twentieth birthday arrived."

Silence settled over the group as we took in everything he'd said. His story explained so much about my past and about why Nysa did so many horrible things, but I didn't feel any relief now that I knew the truth.

Finally, I asked, "How are we supposed to stop the Spirit Goddess?"

"That I don't know," Doran said. "All I know is that this horrible cycle can't continue. We thought we were saving the world, and maybe we did for a short time, but now I fear we've made it even worse."

"Would the Gods be able to divide the Spirit Goddess into two halves again?" Auric asked.

Doran shrugged. "They have the ability, and that was

the deal when I freed them. Will they hold up their end of the bargain? Who knows."

"Then we can't trust them either," Reven said.

"I agree," Doran said. "But right now, we need to focus on defeating Nysa. Otherwise, we won't have to worry about any of that."

Everyone's faces were grim as we prepared for bed. My mates asked me if I was all right, but I didn't know what to say. Doran's words had shaken all of us, making us realize the task ahead of us was much more daunting than we'd realized, and the price of our failure was even higher than we'd imagined.

As I pulled my blanket around me, my eyes stared at the moonlit waves and tried to make sense of it all. We'd reach the Water Realm the next afternoon, thanks to Doran's relentless pace. I was torn between wanting to hurry as much as he did, and wondering if we should stay away, after what we'd learned. The longer we waited, the more chances the Dragons would find us or the new Water Temple first. The sooner we got to the Temple, the sooner I would have to face my mother. The Gods had told me it was my destiny to defeat her, but they hadn't told me everything. By defeating my mother, I would be unleashing something much worse on the world. How could I do that, without some plan to stop the Spirit Goddess?

I'd have to ask the Water God for advice when we spoke to him, except now I wondered if the Gods had been honest with us all along. They could be as twisted as the Goddess, manipulating us to do what they wanted—freeing her.

Things had once been so clear. The Gods were good. The Dragons were evil. Now I realized nothing was as simple as black and white. My mother had a reason for what she'd done, something she and the other Dragons had believed was right. The Gods had their own plans and their own reasons. Even Doran and Enva had motives that might be contrary to what I wanted. The only people I could trust were my mates. I knew in my core they would never betray me, and they would always steer me true. Everyone else wanted something from me. My life. My service. My power.

But I wasn't sure what I wanted anymore, or what the best action was for the entire world. For the first time since this all began, I wasn't certain of my path anymore.

16

AURIC

The Water Realm was connected to the Earth Realm by a bit of land that jutted out in a peninsula, before splitting into hundreds of islands that made up of most of its territory. Doran was taking us on a long route to avoid running into the other Dragons, flying us over turquoise waters and islands with white sands and tall palm trees stretching into the sky.

We took a break at midday after hours of travel. Still in my dragon form, I stretched my wings and devoured some food to combat the aches and exhaustion of flying for days with people and supplies on my back, though I could tell I was getting stronger. Every day my endurance as a Dragon was building, as was my skill at flying. Now if only we could get Slade to fly too. He practiced every morning before we set off and could hover in the air for a few minutes, but anything more than that was still a problem. I wished I could help him in some way, but this was something he had to do on his own.

I spotted Kira standing by herself across the small island, gazing out at the clear blue water with troubled eyes. I trudged over to her and curled up around her with my large scaled body, giving us a hint of privacy from the others. "Are you all right?"

"I'm okay," she said with a smile that looked forced. "Just thinking about what we learned last night."

"It was a lot to take in. So much of what we thought we knew about the Gods was a lie." I'd recorded everything Doran had told us in my journal, which was running out of pages at this point. Every time we spoke with him we learned something new, something which had been lost over time or removed from history purposefully. The other Dragons had kept people living in ignorance and fear, with knowledge restricted to the few. That would not be our legacy.

Kira sighed. "I'm not sure we can trust anything the Gods tell us, and I have no idea what to do about Nysa now. We have to defeat her, but I worry that doing so will only make things worse. And although I still hate her, I understand why she became the person she is now. She thought she was doing what was best for the world but made some bad choices that led her down a dark path. Who's to say we won't do the same?"

I wrapped a golden wing around her. "We'll figure it out. I have faith in you, and we'll be with you through all of it."

ELIZABETH BRIGGS

She ran her hand along my scales slowly. "Thanks. I couldn't do this without the four of you at my side."

"Once we reach the Water Temple, I'll talk to the priests and see if they have any old texts about the Gods. Perhaps we'll find something useful."

"Perhaps," she replied, although she sounded doubtful. I didn't have much hope either, but I had to try.

She leaned against my large side, gazing out at the water again. I wished I could shift back into my human form and hold her, but I still had all the supplies strapped to my back, and we would be leaving soon. Doran would grumble at us if we held the group up by even a minute.

"We'll be at the Water Temple soon at this pace," I said, trying to distract her from her dark thoughts. "Is Reven going to be ready?"

We'd all heard them arguing the night before we went to the Earth Temple, and Reven had never been very amenable to the idea of becoming a Dragon. But he'd also sacrificed himself to save Kira, so we knew he cared for her—even if he didn't want to admit it to himself.

"I think so. Things with him have been...difficult." Her eyes darted to Reven, who stood apart from everyone else, leaning against the palm trees with his arms crossed. As usual, his brooding face made him look like he would rather be anywhere else, unless you noticed that he was turned toward Kira. He always kept an eye on her, even though he tried to make it seem like he didn't care.

I rubbed my head against her side. "I know he'll come around when it's time."

"I wish I had your optimism."

"It's not optimism. I believe in you, and in your other mates." I grinned, giving her a glimpse of my fangs. "And I don't see how Reven could possibly resist you."

She took my large, scaled head in her hands, then pressed a kiss to my forehead. "Thank you. I always feel better after we talk."

Through our bond I did sense that her troubles had lifted slightly. They'd always be there, at least until all of this was over, but they no longer weighed her down quite so much. Good. If I could ease Kira's burden or make her smile, I'd done my duty as her mate.

"Enough standing around," Doran roared, as he flexed his wings. "Do you want to make it to the Water Temple before the Dragons find us? Then let's get moving."

The others grumbled at the shortness of our break while Kira rolled her eyes. I nudged her with my tail. "Come on, let's join the others before your father yells at us again."

"He can be quite annoying, can't he?"

"Sometimes, but he's just looking out for you."

"Is he?" She cast a skeptical eye at him. "You're the only one who seems to trust him."

"I'm trying to give him the benefit of the doubt. I truly think he wants to help us." I flexed my talons and bared my fangs. "But if he turns against us, I'll be ready."

17

KIRA

W e stopped that night at a small fishing village where everyone knew Doran and greeted him warmly—a reaction I'd never seen before. Most people cowered in fear from the Dragons, but he'd flown right into the village and had shifted in front of them. Instead of hiding, people had run out to say hello with smiles on their faces.

"I saved them from a group of elementals a few years ago," Doran explained, as he led us to the small building that served as a tavern and inn for sailors.

"I thought we were supposed to be traveling in secret," I said.

"Trust me, no one from this town will go running to the other Dragons, and it's such a small, inconsequential village none of them will bother coming here."

I glanced across the town, with its wind-battered and

98

sun-bleached buildings, some of which had straw roofs. Palm trees blew lazily overhead, and the air smelled of saltwater and fresh fish from the nearby harbor. Memories of my childhood, living in a place just like this, came rushing back. "This town reminds me of Tidefirth."

"Does it?" Doran asked. "I suppose it is similar."

"Is it possible to go back there?"

"No. Sark burned it down after you left, probably to punish me for making him spare your life. The entire village is little more than ash, along with all the people who once lived there." He rested a hand on my shoulder briefly. "I'm sorry."

Pain gripped my heart. Sark took all those innocent lives...and for what? Some petty rivalry between the two of them? Maybe he and Nysa had started out with good intentions, but they'd done many terrible things over the years too, which couldn't be forgiven. They had to be stopped.

As night fell across the quiet town, I wandered through the small harbor, eyeing the various boats docked there. I spotted Reven sitting on the end of the pier, his legs hanging over the water, the breeze teasing at his black hair. He was so handsome it took my breath away, even after all this time, and I couldn't help but be drawn to him.

He didn't look up as I sat beside him. We sat in silence for a few minutes, simply enjoying the sound of the waves, the feel of the wind, and the way the stars appeared as night crept over the ocean.

His voice finally broke the silence. "The Water Realm brings back old memories."

"Good or bad?" I asked.

"Both."

I nodded, understanding what he meant. "This village reminds me of the place where I grew up. A tiny fishing village like this one. Until Sark came and destroyed it all." I turned toward him, watching the profile of his face. "Where did you grow up in the Water Realm? A town like this?"

He shrugged. "All over."

"You moved around a lot?"

He fell silent, and I worried he wouldn't answer. Reven hated talking about his past. I knew almost nothing about it, and every time I'd tried to ask him, he'd ended the conversation and made it clear he wouldn't say anything more. When he did give me some tidbit about his past, I hoarded it like treasure and pored over it for days. He'd gotten his twin swords from his father. He knew how to sail a boat. His parents were members of the Resistance and had been killed by Sark. But the rest? It was still a mystery.

"I grew up on a ship," Reven said, surprising me.

"Were you a pirate like Doran?" I asked. It would explain the swords and how his father had trained him to use them so expertly.

An amused smirk made Reven even more gorgeous. "No. I was in a traveling carnival, actually."

I blinked at him. Of all the things I'd expected to learn about Reven's past, that was not one of them. "You what?"

"My family's ship was part of a performing troupe that sailed from one island to another, putting on a show in each one."

I had a hard time imagining Reven growing up in such a life. "What kind of performers?"

He shrugged. "Jugglers, acrobats, magicians, animal tamers... We had it all."

"Your family did all that?"

"My parents were known as the Twirling Blades, and they had an act where they danced with their swords, threw knives, and performed other stunts that few could believe." He ran a hand over one of his swords at the memory. "They raised me to be one of them. I never knew any other life. Until Sark took it all away."

"I thought your family was killed because they were in the Resistance."

"They were. Our role as traveling performers made it easy for us to carry messages and to transport or hide people. The carnival was the perfect front for what they were truly doing. I had no idea at the time." His face turned grim. "One day I got into a fight with my parents over something stupid and ran off. I left the boat and went into the city to try to get into trouble. When I got back, all our ships were destroyed. Every single one of them. My parents. My sister. My aunts, uncles, cousins... In one blow, Sark had taken everything I had ever known."

I took his hand and gave it a squeeze. "I'm so sorry."

He kept going, as if he hadn't heard me. "I didn't know what to do. I blamed myself. I told myself if I'd stayed behind, I could have stopped him, or helped some of them escape, or something."

"How old were you?"

"Ten."

"Oh, Reven. There was nothing you could have done. If you were there, Sark would have killed you too."

His hand tightened around mine. "Yes, I know. But the guilt of surviving is hard to get rid of, even if logic tells me there was nothing I could do to save them."

"I understand. I have the same guilt." I leaned my head against his shoulder. "What did you do after that?"

"I fled back into the city, but I knew no one there and had nothing but the clothes on my back and my father's swords, which I'd managed to save from the wreckage. I ended up living on the streets, trying to use my skills to make money, but no one wanted to pay a kid to play with swords. I became a thief in order to survive." He tilted his head back and stared up at the stars. "Turns out those same skills that made my family a good group of performers also made me a good criminal."

"Is that when you become an assassin?"

"No." He scowled and pushed himself to his feet. I could tell by the shuttered look on his face that he was done talking, and probably regretted revealing so much to me. "I think that's enough reminiscing for one night. We have another long day ahead of us tomorrow."

He began to turn away, but I was tired of him always pushing me away. We would be at the Water Temple soon. Something had to change.

I jumped up and caught his arm. "It's fine if you don't want to talk about your past. I know it can be painful. But don't shut me out, please. In a few days we'll be pledging our lives to each other and I have to know that you're serious about this."

"I told you I was." His eyes narrowed and he jerked his arm away. "You want to know how I became an assassin? Fine. I thought I'd spare you the dark details tonight, but since you insist..."

I sighed. "Reven—"

"A man named Harman found me and convinced me to work for him," Reven said, his voice menacing as he spat out the words. "He had a whole gang of street kids and he made us do terrible things. Stealing was the least of it. He sold our bodies to monsters who liked children. He murdered anyone who disobeyed or questioned him. But at least we were fed, and we had each other. I found a new family. A girl."

I wanted to take Reven into my arms and hold him as he spoke about what was obviously a painful tale, but I kept my distance. I worried if I made even the slightest movement, he'd get spooked and run away again.

He stared across the dark waters as he continued. "Her name was Mira. I was fourteen by then, and she was a year younger than me. It was innocent, or as innocent as it could be for two kids who had been forced to grow up way too fast. She was beautiful and kind, and I told her I'd do anything to protect her. When Harman decided he'd sell her off to a man five times her age, we made a plan to run away...but we didn't get far. Harman's men caught her, and she was killed while trying to escape them." His hands clenched at his side. "At the sight of her blood, I lost it and murdered them all with my father's swords. They were the first lives I took.

And then I went back and killed Harman too, along with everyone else I could find. I hunted down every single man and woman he had ever worked with and made sure they'd never prey on children again. That's when the Assassin's Guild invited me to join them." He met my eyes again and spread his arms wide. "And now you know everything. I've been a thief, a whore, and a killer. There's only darkness and death in my past. Forgive me if I don't like talking about it."

Reven's voice was cold and his face was hard, but I could sense the pain inside him. I wrapped my arms around him and held him silently, until some of the tension in his body relaxed and he reluctantly embraced me in return.

"Thank you for telling me," I said. "I'm sorry you went through all that, and I know it must have been difficult to talk about. But your past shaped you into the man you are today. A man I love."

"Don't say that." He took my face in his hands and stared into my eyes. "Don't say those words."

I gazed back at him defiantly. "I'll say them if I want. I don't care if you don't say them in return. But I love you, and I know you care for me too."

"Dammit, woman." He covered my mouth with his and kissed me hard. I melted against him, my curves molding against his strong body, trying to get closer. His tongue glided across my lips, parting them, as his hand gripped the back of my hair to hold me tight. He claimed me with this kiss, branding me as his, showing me how much he cared, even if he couldn't speak it out loud.

When he released my mouth, his voice was rough. "I've

lost everyone I've ever loved. I told myself that love made me weak and swore to never do it again. But when you were kidnapped and that cave fell on me, the only thing that kept me alive was the thought of you. I might not be able to say those words, but I feel it too."

"I know," I said, kissing him over and over. "I know."

Reven may not be able to tell me he loved me, but I knew his heart belonged to me. His face was tormented as he stared down at me, and I ran my thumb across his lips, wishing I could get him to smile. Enough with the bad memories. Maybe I could remind him of some of the good ones now.

"I see now why you're such a good assassin and fighter," I said. "Did you learn anything else while working as a performer? Something fun?"

He looked confused for a second, but then he smirked. "I'm a damn good juggler, actually."

I laughed. "I don't believe it."

He pinned me with a dark look, then retrieved six throwing knives from his belt. With a grace I could never possess he launched them into the air, juggling them back and forth with movements almost too fast to see. If I didn't know better, I'd think he was using air magic as he made the blades fly high, catching them mid-air and throwing them again with the flick of his wrist, before finally collecting them all in one hand and performing an elaborate bow.

I clapped with a big, silly grin on my face. "I have to admit, I'm impressed. And surprised. I never expected that."

He gave me a wink. "What can I say? I'm good with my hands."

"Are you?" I pulled him close, my fingers gripping his black shirt. "I'm going to need a demonstration once we get to the Water Temple."

"I think we can arrange that," he said, before capturing my mouth again, making desire race through me.

Only a few more days, and then Reven would truly be mine.

18

KIRA

Doran's talons hit the sand. "We're here."

I glanced around from where I sat on his back. We'd landed on a small island, barely big enough for the three dragons to stand on together. There were two large rocks, a lone palm tree, and a cluster of seaweed that was being washed on shore. Water surrounded us in every direction, stretching as far as the eye could see.

"What do you mean, we're here?" Jasin asked, his voice gravelly in his dragon form.

"I hate to agree with Jasin, but this doesn't look like a temple," Reven said, from Jasin's back.

Still a dragon, Doran strode to the edge of the island, where the waves met the land. "The Water Temple is below us. We'll have to swim to get there."

I peered down into the crystal blue water but saw nothing. "How do the priests survive living underwater?"

"The Water God protects them," Doran said, as if it was obvious.

"Here's a better question, how are we supposed to get down there?" Jasin asked, shying back from the water before it could touch his claws.

"We'll manage," Doran said. "Auric can shield himself with a bubble of air, while Reven can keep the water away from Jasin. I'll protect Kira. Now, follow me."

He trudged into the water, his wings folding at his side, his tail swishing at the waves. I clutched onto his dark blue scales while Auric and Jasin trailed behind us. Auric didn't seem troubled at all, but Jasin hesitated before entering the ocean. Reven muttered something to him, and the red dragon grumbled and stepped forward into the water.

As soon as Doran slipped below the waves, I held my breath—but found it wasn't necessary. He created a bubble around me by pushing the water back, forming a circle of air that allowed me to breathe. Even though the ocean surrounded us, I remained dry. Doran, on the other hand, didn't seem to need air to breathe underwater. Reven copied him and shielded Jasin as they braved the ocean, while Auric created a similar bubble of air around himself and Slade.

The three dragons walked across the bottom of the ocean, until it sloped down suddenly. The deep water below us was dark, and I couldn't see anything down there. A trickle of fear ran down my spine as I gazed at the vast, deep darkness, filled with the unknown. What if our bubbles gave out? What if something horrible was lurking there?

All I could do was trust my father as he launched himself into the dark depths of the ocean. He sped along the invisible water currents faster than I could have imagined, using his wings to propel him forward. The other two dragons followed, although they were not as fast or as sleek. Doran was in his element, swimming forward into the darkness with no light to guide him. Me, on the other hand, I couldn't see a thing, except for the quick movement of a fish now and then as it darted out of our path. I summoned a bright flame in my palm, but it barely illuminated everything. After a few seconds, I gave up.

Something appeared in the dark depths. A pale glow below us, which Doran led us toward. I caught sight of hundreds of silvery fish dashing back and forth in a cluster stretching far and wide, that almost looked like a busy road. Below them I glimpsed something that looked like the top of a tower, where the glowing light was coming from.

A large, pale structure with towers and turrets slowly revealed itself as we moved deeper. The architecture was intricate, a beautiful thing of swirls and arches that flowed like water itself, somehow looking completely natural rising from the ocean floor. It was impossible to tell how old the building was, but I sensed it had been there a long time.

Doran landed on the bottom of the ocean in front of a giant statue of a dragon at the entrance. As he stepped forward, we passed through a shimmery veil that rippled across my skin. He dropped the water bubble around us, which was no longer needed.

A large dome of air surrounded the Water Temple,

allowing us to breathe safely while we were visiting. Fish swam on the other side and high above us, coming right to the edge of the dome but not entering it. I stared up at it in awe, marveling at the Water God's power.

The other two dragons emerged behind us. Auric created a warm gust of wind that had him dry within seconds, while Jasin shook off the water like a dog as soon as Slade slid off his back. My father didn't seem bothered by the water dripping off him at all.

"This structure looks like it's been here for hundreds of years," Auric said, after returning to his human form. "I thought you said this wasn't the original Water Temple?"

"It's not," Doran said. "Long ago, when I first became a Dragon, there were many temples to the Gods across the four Realms. After Nysa came to power, we imprisoned the Gods in their largest temple, and then had some of the others destroyed. Others naturally became abandoned over the years as people lost faith in their absent Gods. This was one of those temples. The priests have been slowly restoring and preparing it ever since the Water God was freed. When it became clear that Nysa wanted all the temples destroyed, the High Priestess and her mates moved here for safety."

The tall stone door at the front of the temple opened with a loud rumble. A small woman with curly black hair and olive skin stepped through the door. She looked to be a few years older than I was and wore a shimmering blue robe with a necklace made of seashells. With her short height, round face, and warm smile, she was more cute than beautiful, and I instantly felt comfortable around her.

"Kira, this is Opea, the High Priestess of the Water God," Doran said.

Opea bowed low before me. "It is an honor to meet you, and all of the ascendants. We've waited so long for this day."

"The honor is ours," I said.

She turned to my father. "It's good to see you again, Doran."

"You too. How's little Wella?"

"Walking now and a real nuisance," Opea said with a laugh. "Please, come inside. We have food and refreshments and have prepared some rooms for you."

We stepped into a large entry room with walls the color of pale sand and shiny sea green tiles on the floor. Four handsome men waited for us, and Opea introduced us to her priests. One of them held a squirming toddler with the same round face as Opea but lighter hair, who I guessed was Wella.

Opea escorted me to a bedroom, while the priests took the men in a different direction. As soon as the door to the room opened, I gasped. Inside was a bed larger than any I had seen before, easily wide enough for me and all my mates.

"Does this meet your needs?" Opea asked.

"It does. I've never seen such a grand bed before. How long have you been waiting for us?"

"We've been ready for months now, ever since Doran informed us it was time to abandon the old temple. We weren't sure how soon you would visit us, but we've been prepared." She gave me a calm, pleasant smile. "Now please, rest and relax as much as you need. There's a washroom attached to this room for your convenience, and I'll have food sent up for you. Your mates are staying in rooms down the hall. The bonding room is ready for you, but there's no rush. You're welcome to take a few days to recover first, if you'd like. We're quite safe down here."

"Thank you," I said. Rest sounded nice. I felt like I could sleep for days, but then I remember Reven's heated kiss. "I'd prefer to do the bonding sooner than later."

"Of course," she said, with a knowing wink. "When you're ready, you can proceed to the bonding room from the door in the back of the great hall."

She bowed once and then left me alone in the large, elegant room. The same curved lines from the temple were reflected here in the furniture, and the fabrics were soft and luxurious in colors of white, gray, and aqua blue. Glittering seashells and dried starfish served as decorations, along with a fern that looked like it should be growing off the ocean floor.

I moved to the washroom, where I found a large round pool with clear blue water, which I realized was a natural spring that fed in from outside the temple. The water was cooler than I liked, but I used my fire magic to warm it up, and then stripped off my clothes and settled inside. The pool was big enough that my mates and I could all sit in it, and I allowed myself to stretch out and float on my back as the warm water melted away all the dirt and tension from traveling over the last few days.

For the first time in ages, I felt safe. No one could find us here, deep beneath the waves. I didn't have to constantly look over my shoulder and prepare for a possible attack. The temple wasn't in ruins or filled with death, and we didn't have to hurry.

I only wished this peace could last.

19

REVEN

A fter washing up and changing into fresh clothes, I sought out Kira's bedroom. I knocked sharply and she called for me to enter. When I stepped inside, I caught a glimpse of her pulling a light green robe around her body. Memories of the last time I'd seen her naked came rushing back. Her skin glistening with sweat as she was pressed between Jasin and Auric. Her soft curves as they ran their hands over her. Her full lips as they opened for me...

"Are you ready?" she asked. Her hair was still damp, making it a darker red than normal, and her face was flushed with life. She looked too damn beautiful to be real.

I'd been resistant to this bonding thing from the beginning. I hadn't wanted to be one of Kira's mates, or the next Azure Dragon, or the Water's God's chosen one. Even once I'd accepted my fate and grown to care for Kira, the idea of having sex with her in some ritual felt so...forced. Everyone in the temple would be waiting for us to get on with it, knowing exactly what we were doing the entire time. We might as well be on display. But now that she was standing in front of me, her eyes full of hope and desire, her body naked under that robe?

I was ready.

I yanked her toward me and took her mouth, hard. She let out a little noise of surprise as my lips moved across hers and my tongue slipped inside. She melted against me immediately as we kissed, the perfect size and shape to fit against me, and my hands couldn't help but seek out her bare skin. I tugged open her robe and gripped her hip, holding her in place as I angled her head to kiss her deeper. Gods, she tasted good. Before Kira, kissing had never been something I cared about. Now I could do it for hours and never grow tired of feeling her lips against mine.

She drew back slightly and met my eyes. "We're supposed to do this in the bonding room."

"I've never been good at following rules."

I dragged her mouth back to mine, pulling her tight against me, so that her hard nipples brushed against the fabric of my shirt and the bulge of my cock pressed between her thighs. She let out a throaty hum of desire, and I ground myself against her, driving us both a little mad with need.

My hand slid down her hip and dipped between her thighs, finding her wet and pulsing for me. I stroked her once and she widened her legs in response, while her fingers curled into my shirt like she was trying to stop me from pulling away. I wanted to tell her there was no chance of that, but my mouth was devouring hers and my fingers were exploring the silky, swollen folds she'd offered to me.

When I glided into that tight wet heat, she let out a moan against my lips. Her thighs tightened, trapping my hand between them, while I slid in and out of her slowly. With my other hand I held her up, knowing her knees would be weak when I was through with her. I slipped another finger inside and rubbed her clit at the same time, feeling her tense around me. Knowing how close she was already encouraged me to move faster and deeper, forcing her to rock her hips in time with my movements, her arms tightening around my neck for support. She cried out my name into my mouth as the climax swept over her, her body turning to liquid against me.

I slowly removed my fingers and held her until she could stand on her own again. "Told you I was good with my hands."

"You weren't kidding." Her eyes were dazed as she closed her robe and tied it.

I took her hand in mine. "Let's find this bonding room."

The hallway and the great room were both empty, much to my relief. The hour must be late, though it was hard to tell deep below the ocean, where sunlight couldn't reach. I certainly wasn't tired—no, my body was full of energy, the same rush I got when I was about to slit someone's throat from the shadows or leap into a fight. The anticipation only made what was coming even sweeter.

The door to the bonding room opened easily at my touch. The first thing I saw was the floor-to-ceiling opening to the ocean on one side. The dome must end right there because fish swam just outside, and we could almost reach out and touch them. Coral and seaweed lined the ocean floor, and I caught a glimpse of an eel poking its head out of some rocks.

A raised path led from the door to a large bed, and around this platform was a shallow pool of water, only knee-high. The pool's floor was covered in shining seashells that caught the flickering candlelight around the room.

"It's beautiful," Kira whispered.

One of the other guys would have told her she was even more beautiful or something, but I wasn't good at this romance crap. I'd never had a real relationship. I hated talking about my feelings. And sex? Sex was always for a purpose. Making money. Getting information. Relieving stress. Never for love.

Until now.

I grabbed Kira around the waist, feeling her curves under that thin robe, and picked her up, wrapping her legs around me. She let out an excited laugh, then settled into my arms as I carried her to the bed. I set her down on her back and grabbed her wrists, pinning them to the bed. I loomed over her body, caging her in, giving her no way to escape.

"Now you're mine," I said.

She looked up at me with open desire and complete trust. "What are you going to do with me?"

Her robe had fallen open and I raked my eyes down her body. "Everything."

My gaze lingered on her full breasts and narrow hips, before dipping down to that triangle between her legs, already wet from my touch. Damn, she was stunning. Why had I resisted her so long?

That was over now. She was impossible to resist, and I was done trying to fight it.

Still holding her wrists, I bent my head to those perfect round breasts and flicked my tongue across her hard nipple. She arched her back in response, begging for more, and I sucked one of those dark buds into my mouth. The soft moan from her lips turned me on even more, as did the taste of her. I'd never considered myself a lucky man, but I was starting to change my mind about that.

I worshipped each breast until she was begging and writhing under me, desperate for more. An overwhelming need to be inside her took over, and I released her wrists so I could tear off my clothes. Her eager fingers reached up to help me, her eyes hungry as I removed my shirt and tossed it aside. The rest of my clothes hit the floor, and then I moved over her again.

"I never thought this moment would come," she said, as she gazed up at me.

The intensity of her eyes was too much. She wrecked me, and I was going to fall apart if she kept that up. The urge to claim her as my own grew too strong to ignore, and I couldn't wait a second longer. I grabbed her waist and flipped her over onto her stomach, making her gasp. I yanked her hips up so they were level with mine, and then I rammed myself deep inside.

She let out the most beautiful scream I'd ever heard as I filled her from behind, the sound echoing throughout the room. I grit my teeth at the feel of her tight, damp heat. My hand wrapped around her thick red hair, tugging her head back, forcing me deeper inside. I arched over her to press my lips to her neck, and she trembled under my touch.

"I have a secret," I said into her ear, as I held her there. Not moving yet, just enjoying the feel of her body squeezed tight around my cock.

"Only one?"

I nipped at her shoulder. "I think you know all the rest by now."

"Tell me," she said, her voice husky.

"I've never done this before with anyone I actually cared about."

With that, I began to move. I rocked into her with hard, rough thrusts, and she pushed her hips back at me, taking me deeper. With one hand gripping her hair and the other on her hip, I completely controlled her body, forcing her to accept whatever I gave her.

I took her hard and rough, slamming into her again and again, and her moans of pleasure only grew louder. I reached between her thighs to find her clit, and each time I pushed forward, my fingers rubbed against her there. She tightened around me, her body close to the edge, and I was right there with her. I'd thought I was claiming her, but she was the one taking everything from me and still demanding more—and I wanted to give it to her. Not just tonight or in the bedroom, but for the rest of our lives.

I felt it when she came apart. Every wet inch of her clenched around me, and it felt so good I couldn't stop the pleasure from cresting over me too. Water shot into the air around us, while ice spread across our skin, locking us together. I buried my face in her neck, inhaling her, while our bodies rocked together through it all.

The ice melted away and the water sank back into the pool around us. I kissed the back of her neck, as I pulsed inside her, before gathering her in my arms and lowering us to the bed. How had I ever lived without Kira? She made me feel so damn alive.

"I love you," I said, the words slipping out of me. I couldn't stop them anymore. I didn't want to.

She touched my face and smiled. "I know."

20

KIRA

I must have dozed off in Reven's arms, because at the sound of rushing water my eyes snapped open. I yanked my robe up around me, covering my naked skin. Reven sat up and shoved me behind him, protecting me with his body. Water poured into the dome in front of us, and I worried that the entire thing would crash down and crush us under the weight.

The water rushing in began to take shape, forming a large body with four legs, a long tail, a head with a pointed snout, and great wings that rose upon its back. A huge dragon arose in front of us, a creature of pure swirling water with glowing white eyes and fangs made of ice shards.

"The final binding is complete at last," the Water God said.

I reached for my magic, finding the fluid grace of water deep inside me alongside the other three elements, and summoned a snowball in my palm. A large smile spread across my face as it slowly melted against my fingertips. We'd done it. I was bound to each of my mates now, able to use all four elements, along with my own life magic.

"Can I turn into a dragon now?" I asked aloud.

"Not yet," the Water God said. "Not until the Spirit Goddess gives you her blessing."

"The Spirit Goddess is trapped inside Nysa," Reven said dryly. "Something the other Gods failed to mention."

The great dragon flexed his watery wings. "When you defeat Nysa, our Goddess will be freed. Only then will you be able to unlock your true powers."

"But if we free her, the Death Goddess will turn this world into another realm of the dead," I said.

The glowing eyes narrowed. "Doran told you this, but he is also the one who imprisoned us for nearly a thousand years. Nysa and her mates wanted unending power and immortal life. Now they lie to spread doubt through your hearts."

I glanced at Reven warily. "Is it true that the Spirit Goddess is actually the twin Goddesses of Life and Death, bound together?"

"That is true. One cannot exist without the other. Life and death. Dark and light. There must be balance."

"If we free her and the balance shifts too much to one side, can the Gods help us split the Spirit Goddess apart and banish the Death Goddess from this world?"

"We can. If it comes to that, we will."

I nodded. It was the most we could ask for.

The dragon's tail swished back and forth in the low pool. "Do not forget that to defeat Nysa, Doran must be destroyed first. He will tell you anything to protect himself and his mate. You cannot trust him."

That was true, but could we trust the Gods either? I wasn't sure. "I understand."

"The time of the Black Dragon is over, and now the ascendants must rise. Do not fail us."

The Water God began to flow back into the dome, losing shape, but Reven called out, "Wait!"

The huge dragon paused, reforming instantly, and asked, "Yes?"

Reven's brow furrowed. "Why me? I'm not a hero. I didn't want this. I rejected my fate at every turn. You must have known I would, but you picked me anyway."

"The Fire God looks for courage. The Air God chooses one with wisdom. The Earth God seeks out stability. I value change."

"Change?" Reven asked.

"Adaptability. Resourcefulness. A certain fluidity in morals. The world is never as simple as black and white or right and wrong. It is always shifting, and my Dragon shifts with it. I did not want a hero. I wanted someone who would survive, and change, and grow, and show the ascendant how to do the same."

"I see..." Reven said, although he sounded more confused than ever. I reached for his hand and gave it a squeeze. I was certain he was the perfect person to be the next Azure Dragon and my mate, even if he wasn't. He'd made me wait and doubt and nearly tear my hair out plenty of times, but that had only made it even better when he'd finally admitted his feelings for me. Jasin and Auric had loved me from the start, but Slade and Reven had made me work for it—and I'd learned something from each of them. I couldn't have gotten to this point with Reven if not for the other men, and I saw now how each one complemented me and made me become a better person. Including Reven.

"Trust in the Gods," the dragon said. "We created you. We chose you. And we have reasons for everything we do."

With that, he collapsed with a huge splash, and was gone. I had to give the Gods credit, they were good at dramatic entrances and exits.

Reven turned toward me and slid his hand around my waist, bringing me back to him. "Now that that's done, it's time for round two."

I couldn't help but laugh as he pulled open my robe and eased me back onto the bed. "Is that so?"

"I've waited a long time for this night. The other men have been with you multiple times, but we have some catching up to do. I'm not letting you go until I've explored every inch of you. Multiple times."

His head bent to my chest and he ran his tongue in the valley between my breasts, making me gasp. For once, I didn't have to rush off after speaking with a God. No one was waiting for us or coming to attack us. We could spend the entire night in the bonding room if he wanted.

And as Reven kissed his way down my body, I had a feeling he wasn't in any rush to leave either.

21

KIRA

In the morning we met for breakfast with the others in a dining room with windows that looked out to the ocean. Opea and her priests served us fruit and pastries, which they said they traded for when they visited a nearby island once a week. I didn't question it too much. Despite the remote locations of the temples, the Gods always found a way to provide for their priests somehow.

As Opea and her priests left so that we could have privacy, I thought of Calla, the High Priestess of the Fire God, and wondered how she and her mates were doing. The last time I'd seen her had been in the capital of the Air Realm, but I wasn't sure if she planned to stay in Stormhaven until it was safe for her to return to her temple. Sark was her grandfather and he'd kept my presence a secret in exchange for Doran keeping quiet about her. Did that mean Sark actually cared about Calla in some way? I'd always assumed he was heartless, but maybe even the worst Dragons had something or someone they cared about.

I gazed across the table at my father. Was I his weakness too? Or was he playing me this entire time?

Reven must have seen my troubled look because he reached under the table and gave my thigh a squeeze, reminding me of our night together. My worries melted away, and I gave him a grateful smile.

"I'm guessing the bonding went well," Jasin said with a smirk as he took his seat across from me.

"How can you tell?" I asked.

Slade began to load up his plate with food. "You look content. Less troubled."

I smiled and looked down at the plate in front of me as color flooded my cheeks. "I suppose I am. Everything feels like it's as it should be."

"Now that you've bonded with all of us, what is the next step?" Auric asked, as he folded a napkin across his lap.

I sighed. "I can access all of your powers now, but the Water God told me I can't become a dragon myself until the Spirit Goddess blesses me. Which could prove difficult."

"You need to confront Nysa," Doran said, before popping a piece of melon into his mouth. "I suggest we do it at the Spirit Temple near Soulspire, since that's where the blessing needs to take place."

"Somehow I doubt the other Dragons will let us just walk in there," Reven said.

Doran nodded. "Once they learn you've obtained all four elemental powers, they'll know you're heading for the

Spirit Temple next. I would expect it to be heavily defended with both shades and soldiers from the Onyx Army, along with the Dragons themselves."

"We'll never get in there," Jasin muttered.

"Not alone, no," Doran said.

I picked at the food in front of me as I considered. "We need to call upon our allies."

"What allies?" Reven said. "We have the Resistance, who just lost their leader and... Oh wait, that's it."

"I can speak with my father," Auric said. "He has no love for the Dragons but was scared to turn against them. I might be able to convince him to change his mind, if I explain how close we are to defeating them. Perhaps he could lend us some of his soldiers."

Jasin arched an eyebrow at me. "What about that bandit gang you were once a member of, Kira? Would they help us?"

I took a long sip of orange juice. "Cadock's men? I asked before and he said no, but it couldn't hurt to try again. We are desperate, after all."

Reven rolled his eyes. "They'll never say yes. I'd have better luck convincing the Assassin's Guild to join us."

"Do you think you could?" I asked.

He opened and closed his mouth, then scowled. "Maybe. They might do it if we paid them well."

Jasin dragged a hand through his auburn hair. "Even if they all said yes, which is unlikely, it still won't be enough."

I glanced between my father and my mates, then spoke

the idea that had been brewing in my head for some time. "We need to ask the elementals to help us."

"The elementals?" Doran asked with a sharp laugh. "Why would they ever agree to that?"

"The elementals hate the Dragons and the shades, according to Enva," I said. "They might be willing to side with us if we explain that we're planning to defeat them."

Jasin shook his head. "Just because you saved one elemental doesn't mean they'll fight beside us."

I shrugged. "It can't hurt to ask."

"It can if they attack us."

"He's right, it's a big risk," Slade said. "Even asking them to help could be dangerous."

"We have to try," I said. "Humans think the elementals are our enemies. Elementals think the same of us. But it doesn't have to be that way. There were times when our two kinds were at peace."

"You think you can unite elementals and humans and erase hundreds of years of hatred and fear?" Reven asked.

"Not overnight, no. But this would be a good first step. I just want to talk to them. I know it's dangerous, but we need them. I don't think we can do this without their help."

Auric drummed his fingers on the table with a thoughtful expression. "How would you even contact the elementals? There are different types of them spread across the world."

"They have a capital, of sorts, past the Fire Realm," Doran said. "There's a council of leaders, one from each type of elemental. I could take you there."

"Won't they be suspicious if we show up with one of the Dragons we're planning to replace?" I asked.

"So I'll keep out of sight," he said with a shrug.

"There's another problem with this plan," Auric said. "It'll take a long time to visit all these different groups and try to convince them to help us."

I glanced between everyone at the table, weighing the options, before saying, "We'll have to split up. Slade will go to the Resistance, Auric will speak with his father, Reven will ask the Assassin's Guild, and Jasin will try to convince the bandits. Doran and I will find the elementals."

Jasin shook his head with a frown. "I don't like the idea of splitting up."

"Especially if it means none of us will be with you to protect you," Slade said.

"I'll keep her safe," Doran said. "You have my word."

"But can we trust your word?" Reven asked.

Doran's eyes narrowed. "I would never do anything to harm my daughter. Surely you know that by now. Have I not done everything I said I would?"

"Forgive us for being cautious," Auric said. "We're just trying to make sure Kira stays safe."

I pinched the bridge of my nose, fighting off an oncoming headache, probably from the stress of this combined with the lack of sleep. "I know this plan isn't ideal, but this is the only way. The longer we take, the longer the Dragons can prepare to stand against us. We have to recruit allies, and we have to do it quickly. We must split up, even if it puts all of us in danger." My voice softened as I looked at each of them. "I'll have Doran, and I can control all four elements now. You don't need to worry about me."

Slade reached for my hand. "We always will worry."

"It's settled then." Doran pressed his palms on the table and stood. "But before we rush off to the four corners of the world, you each need more training first. Meet me in the courtyard in an hour."

After he was gone, Reven fixed me with a dark look. "You know you can't trust him."

"I don't trust him," I said, remembering the Water God's comments last night. "But he has kept his word so far, and he's helped us a lot. We would never have found this temple without him. He might betray us in the end, but we'll be prepared if he does."

Slade rubbed his beard. "I have another idea. I've been wondering if it's possible to imbue a weapon with all of our magic."

"How would that work?" Jasin asked.

"I'm not sure, but it might be effective against Nysa once we've defeated her mates, or perhaps even against the Spirit Goddess." Slade shrugged. "I'd like to try, but I'd need my forge."

"We could plan to reconvene in your village," Auric said.

The plan was set. Now we just had to find a way to pull it off.

22

JASIN

Doran waited for us in front of the temple, where he leaned against the large dragon statue. He stared at the fish swimming outside the dome and something in his expression reminded me of Kira. She often got lost in her thoughts too, especially when something was weighing heavily on her mind, which was often lately. Although after her night with Reven she was smiling a little easier, at least. A few days of peace and rest at the Water Temple would be good for her too, even if I was itching to get moving and take action.

Doran heard us approach and turned toward us. "Good, you're all here." He moved to stand before us and scrutinized us in turn. "If you're going to fight the Dragons in a few weeks, you'll need to be better prepared. Right now, you're not even close to being ready. I'm amazed you've survived this long, honestly."

"Great speech," I mumbled. "I feel so inspired now."

Reven smirked beside me, while Doran shot me a sharp look before continuing. "Today we're going to focus on opposing elements. Each element has a direct opposite—fire and water, earth and air, life and death. As I mentioned before, this is how we imprisoned the Gods, using the element they were weakest against. You'll be strongest when fighting someone with opposing magic, whether it's a Dragon or an elemental, but you'll also be at your weakest. I want you to pair up—Reven with Jasin, Auric with Slade—and practice blocking each other's magical attacks."

"And me?" Kira asked.

"You and I will start your water magic training today."

Reven and I moved to the other side of the courtyard, both of us wearing matching scowls. Maybe we were supposed to be opposites, but sometimes I thought I had more in common with him than I did with the others. I hadn't liked the guy at first, but now we had an unspoken understanding. And we both seemed to feel the same way about Doran.

"I should be the one training her in water," Reven growled, once we were out of earshot.

I snorted. "Now that her perfect father is here, she doesn't need us for that anymore."

We took up positions facing each other and summoned our magic. I threw a ball of fire at Reven, but he met it with a blast of water and they both sizzled out.

"She's going to be heartbroken when his true colors emerge," I said, as Reven threw shards of ice my way. I put up a wall of fire to block them, melting them before they could hit me.

"And we'll be there to comfort her."

"Unless we're all split up." My jaw clenched as I formed a sword made entirely of fire and lunged at him. I hated this plan we'd come up with. Leaving her alone with Doran was a bad idea, but she wouldn't listen to reason about it.

Reven formed a shield of water and blocked me, then let the water reform into two daggers, which he threw at me. I knocked one away, but the other grazed my arm, making me flinch.

I rubbed the small cut, which burned with cold. "Nice one."

Reven nodded at my compliment. "The Assassin's Guild headquarters are on the way to the Fire Realm and not far from here. I can take care of business there quickly and then follow Kira and Doran from a distance. If I feel anything through the bond, I'll be able to get to Kira fast."

"That would make me feel a lot better about this plan. Do you think he'll try something?"

"No, but I like to be prepared for anything."

"Me too. And even if he isn't a threat to her, the elementals could be."

"Exactly."

Doran walked over to us while we shot more fire and water at each other. "How are you both doing with this?"

"Fine," Reven said.

"I will say, I'm impressed," Doran said. "The two of you haven't known each other long, but you don't seem to hate each other. Sark and I..." His face twisted. "Let's just say it took a long time before we could work together."

"That isn't a problem for us," Reven said.

"No, and not for Slade and Auric either it seems."

"We're a team," I said, puffing up my chest a little. "Brothers united with a shared cause—protecting and loving Kira. Whatever personal issues we had with each other, we've managed to get past them."

"So I've seen." Doran rubbed his chin, his eyes thoughtful. "Nysa's mates and I can barely stand to be in the same room as each other. We've never been very good at working as a team, and the bond chafes at us after all these years. Blocking the other Dragons out was the only way I could stay sane. But things are different with all of you—and that's how you'll defeat the other Dragons."

I couldn't imagine hating Kira's other mates like that. Sure, we'd had our differences at first. We'd gotten into fights. We'd questioned each other's loyalties. But in the end, we'd united under our shared love of Kira and our common purpose of defeating the Dragons. All I had to do was reach for the bond with Kira and I felt her mates there too. Auric was the strongest, like a sunny breeze brushing against my mind, and I'd started to feel Slade's cool, stony presence recently. Now that Reven had bonded with Kira there was a new awareness too, a tiny cool flicker that I knew would quickly grow into more.

Doran spent a few minutes showing us how to imprison the other person with our element, and then Reven practiced encasing me in ice, sometimes just my feet so I couldn't dodge his attacks, and sometimes my entire body. I did the same with Reven, surrounding him with flames, and at one point making him yelp. Across the courtyard, Slade and Auric were practicing similar tactics with their own magic. I had a feeling we'd need some healing from Kira after this was all over.

"I think that's enough for now," Doran called out, sometime later. "We're going to practice again over the next few days, using different combinations, until you're used to fighting every kind of magic. Slade, I want you to also spend some time practicing your flying. You're almost there, and we need you to be ready before we depart. Reven, you should do that too. And all of you should work on building your bonds with Kira and each other. That will be the key to winning against the other Dragons."

With that, he dismissed us and went back into the Temple. A grin spread across my face, despite my weariness and pain in all the places Reven had hit me. I knew exactly how I wanted to work on strengthening our bonds. And I had a feeling the other guys wouldn't mind either.

23

KIRA

As I prepared for bed after a long day of training with Doran, I heard a knock. I opened my door and found Jasin, Auric, and Reven standing outside, each one so handsome it made my pulse race.

Jasin leaned against the doorway and gave me a sinful smile. "I thought you could use some company tonight, so I invited the others. Doran did tell us to work on building our bond, after all."

"Yes, he did." Excitement fluttered inside my stomach as I gestured for them to come inside. Memories of the last time the four of us shared an evening together came rushing back, and I could only hope for another night like that. "I was about to take a bath. You should all join me."

"I invited Slade too," Jasin said, as they stepped inside.

My eyebrows darted up. "Did you? That was kind, but I doubt he'll join us."

He shrugged. "You never know. I think he'll surprise you."

"This bed is enormous," Auric said, pushing his hand on it. "We'll definitely have to take advantage of this later."

"This bath is too," Reven said from the other room.

"A suite built for a Dragon and her mates," I said, as I followed Reven's voice.

Jasin dipped his hand in the bath. "Oh yes, this is definitely my favorite temple."

My men quickly removed their clothes and I took in Auric's tall frame, Jasin's abundance of muscles, and Reven's toned physique. Each one of them was already hard and ready for me, and at that moment I knew I was the luckiest woman in the world.

They stepped into the pool, which Jasin had heated to the perfect temperature to soothe away any aches and pains from today's lessons. I dropped my robe, baring myself before them, and they gazed up at me as I slipped into the bath beside them. My men wasted no time in circling me, their eyes hungry, their intentions clear. Jasin's mouth found mine first, his lips warm against mine, before Reven dragged my face toward him to kiss me next. Auric's arms circled me from behind, and I turned my head to taste his lips too. Their naked, wet bodies surrounded me, sliding against my bare skin, and desire raced through my veins.

The three of us had done this before, but now it was different because I could sense Reven through the bond. With every touch and kiss, his presence in my mind grew stronger. I no longer had to wonder if he loved me or if he would ever open up—he had given himself to me completely last night, and all my doubts about him had vanished.

I heard footsteps and looked up to see Slade standing on the edge of the bath. "You're here," I whispered.

Slade shrugged. "Jasin invited me."

"Told you," Jasin said with a wink.

"And you're okay with this?" I asked.

"The idea of sharing you doesn't bother me anymore, not like it did." Slade tugged off his shirt and tossed it aside, revealing that dark, muscular chest that just begged to be touched. "I'd like to try."

"Really?" I asked, my heart skipping a beat in anticipation.

He slid down his trousers and stepped into the bath. He was already hard as steel, which made me think he might be telling the truth. "I want to do whatever makes you happy, and I can tell this does. I admit, I'm a little curious too."

I wrapped my arms around his neck and kissed him to show how much this meant to me. "We'll go slow and you don't have to do anything you don't want."

He chuckled softly, his voice low and delicious. "I can handle it."

He leaned back against the edge of the bath, spreading his arms wide. I nestled up against him, kissing his bearded neck, running my hands along his shoulders and his strong chest, down to his hard cock. I took it in hand, enjoying the way it filled up my palm, as I kissed him again.

But I couldn't neglect my other mates either. I turned and faced them, but Slade's arms wrapped around me, pulling my behind up against his hips. He held me against him, his cock nestled between my cheeks, his hands on my breasts. I leaned back on his chest and turned my head to kiss him, while the other men watched us with rapt expressions.

They moved forward through the water, drawing closer to me as if they couldn't resist. Jasin and Auric took up position on either side of me, kissing my shoulders, my neck, and the curves of my breasts, while I rested against Slade's chest. Reven claimed the middle, and he dipped under the water with a filthy expression that made my breath catch. He spread my legs wide, and then his mouth moved between my thighs, his tongue darting out to flick against me. I cried out and wove my fingers in his black hair under the water. He stayed down there, licking and sucking on me without coming up for air, using the fact that he could breathe underwater to my advantage. With each touch of his mouth and stroke of his tongue I came apart more and more, while Jasin and Auric took turns claiming my lips and Slade's strong body held me in place.

But it wasn't enough. I dragged Reven up out of the water and captured his mouth with mine, greedy for more of him. His hard body pressed against me, pinning me between him and Slade. I wrapped my hand around his behind and pulled his hips against me. His cock slid easily inside me, exactly where it belonged, and he let out a low, sensual groan.

Auric and Jasin moved to the sides of the bath to watch, while Reven began to pump into me. He grabbed onto my hips to get better leverage, while Slade's hands cupped my breasts and pinched my nipples. Every time Reven thrust into me he pushed me back against Slade, who grunted as his cock rubbed between my cheeks. I wanted him inside me too, but wasn't sure Slade was ready for that level of sharing yet. He was already doing so much more than I ever thought he would. I turned my head and studied his face, observing the hunger in his eyes, before his lush lips came down on mine again.

Slade dipped a hand between me and Reven, finding my clit and stroking it. The water surged around us and I clutched Reven's shoulders with one hand and touched Slade's face with the other, letting them control my body completely. I never felt more cherished than when I was squeezed between two of my mates, and I sensed their passion and love through the bond like a warm glow in my chest. The orgasm crested over me like a wave and swept Reven along with it, making him groan and push deeper inside me with his release. He rested his head against my shoulder, his arms wrapped around me, while Slade held both of us steady.

I kissed Reven slowly, then turned my head to kiss Slade next. "Was that all right?"

"More than all right," Slade said. "I want to watch you with all of them."

"I think they'll be happy to oblige," Reven said with a grin, as he moved to the other side of the tub to watch the next round.

Jasin took Reven's place immediately and gripped my

chin in his hand before kissing me hard. He spun me around so I straddled Slade, while he shoved my wet hair aside and kissed the back of my neck. I wrapped my arms around Slade and my lips found his, while Jasin cupped my breasts and squeezed them roughly.

I felt Jasin's cock against my thighs, and then he slid into me from behind with one deep thrust, making me gasp into Slade's mouth. Jasin began to rock into me, sliding me against Slade with each movement. Slade's hard length pressed between us, pulsing with need, but it wasn't his turn yet. He took it in his hand and began rubbing it against my clit, sending sparks throughout my entire core.

I threw my head back and held onto Slade tightly as the two of them stroked me from different angles, making my desire rise higher and higher. I was caged between my two strongest mates, trapped between their muscular bodies, and I gave myself up to them completely. My climax hit me hard and fast, like flint striking steel and sparking a bonfire. Jasin rode me harder and deeper, his movements rough and fast as he pounded into me, and then he exploded too.

He leaned against my back and kissed my neck, while Slade claimed my mouth again. I knew Slade had to be close from the way his cock pulsed against me, but he didn't seem to be in any hurry. He actually seemed to be enjoying this, which still surprised me.

After Jasin moved away, Auric took my hand. "Come. Let's try out that giant bed of yours."

He helped me out of the water, dried me off with a quick gust of warm air, and led me into the bedroom. My other mates followed as Auric and I sank onto the massive bed, and they spread out around us. Auric and I kissed and stroked each other, but then I moved over to Slade's body, needing to touch his hard length after being teased by it for so long. Auric grabbed my behind as I crawled across the bed, lifting it up as he got in position behind me.

Slade watched everything that was happening intently with his hands folded behind his head, his dark cock standing straight up at attention. I brought my head down and kissed the tip of it, while Auric lined himself up. Slade groaned, and I swirled my tongue around the head of his cock, as Auric gripped my hips and began to push inside slowly. I took Slade into my mouth inch by inch and let out a low hum of approval as both men entered me at the same time.

I looked up to see Jasin and Reven watching us, which only excited me more. One of Slade's hands came down to grip my hair, his hips arching up slightly off the bed, making me take more of him. At the same time, Auric slid deeper into me from behind, filling me up and stretching me wide, before he finally bottomed out inside.

Auric began to move, pulling out slowly before thrusting deep again, and I pushed back against him to take even more. He felt so deep and big back there it was almost too much, yet I still wanted more. Slade filled my mouth completely, and I used my hands to work his shaft as I sucked on him. He'd given me so much tonight by joining us, and I wanted to give him something in return.

The three of us found a rhythm, with Auric rocking me

forward and making me take Slade deeper between my lips. Jasin and Reven moved in on either side of me and began kissing and stroking my breasts, my stomach, and that spot between my legs that begged for attention.

The touch of all four of my mates at once was the most incredible feeling, and another orgasm shuddered through me, this one stronger than all the others. It seemed to go on for an eternity, filling my entire body with pleasure. Slade's fingers tightened in my hair and he groaned, his hips thrusting up at me faster as his seed spilled into my mouth. That sent Auric over the edge too, and he slid deep inside me one last time as his own release came.

I fell onto the bed between Slade and Auric, while Jasin and Reven moved over me. I kissed each of them one by one, feeling their love through the bond, which had grown stronger in the last few minutes. If we kept this up, we would be unstoppable.

24

KIRA

W e spent a week at the Water Temple, which was good for everyone. We hadn't had a chance to rest since we'd visited Slade's village, and while there we were constantly worried the Dragons would show up and attack. Down here we could truly relax, although we did miss sunshine and fresh air and were all starting to get a little sick of eating fish at every meal.

My mates and I spent our days training with Doran and discussing strategies for the battle at the Spirit Temple. And our nights...we spent those strengthening our bonds together, both as a group and one on one. Sometimes I would share a bed with only one of my mates, since I sensed that they needed their alone time with me. On other nights, two of them would join me in bed. And on our last night together, they all did, taking turns to please me over and over.

And then it was time to leave.

We stood outside the temple, with all of our supplies packed and ready to go. Opea moved forward and embraced me. "Good luck on your journey. We shall be praying for your success."

"Thank you for everything," I said.

Opea's handsome priests bowed before us, while her daughter clung to her skirts and peered out at me. I'd considered asking for their help at the Spirit Temple, since Opea had been blessed with magic from her God like the other High Priestesses, but I was too worried about her young daughter growing up without a mother.

I turned toward my mates and was immediately swept up into Jasin's arms. He gave me a kiss so full of passion that my cheeks grew red at the thought of my father watching us. I laughed and pushed him back. "I'll miss you too, Jasin."

"Be careful," he said, before stepping away.

Auric embraced me next, before giving me a warm kiss that was a lot less embarrassing but still wonderful. He'd spent much of his free time scouring the temple's library, but he hadn't been able to find any real information about the Spirit Goddess. "I'll be counting down the days until we meet again."

"Me too."

Slade gave me a strong hug next, his muscular arms squeezing me hard. I was so proud of him—Slade had worked day and night to practice flying alongside Reven, and Doran had decided they were both ready to travel. I pressed a soft kiss to his lips, and then he rested his forehead against mine as he simply held me close.

"Come back to us," he said.

"I will."

Reven was last and he stepped forward slowly, then took my face in his hands and kissed me hard. "I'll see you soon. Watch your back."

His words were casual, but I knew what he meant. "I love you too," I whispered to him.

He gave me a wry smirk, before stepping back. My chest tightened as I stared at the four of them, wishing we didn't have to be apart for so long. But my bond with each of them was stronger than ever, and even though we'd be far away, we'd still be together.

My mates said goodbye to each other next, while I turned toward my father. He was already in his dragon form, and one of Opea's priests had fastened some of our supplies to his back. He swung his head toward me. "Are you finally done with your tearful goodbyes?"

"There were no tears," I said, as I climbed onto his back. He snorted, and then we watched as my mates transformed too. As they stood before me, four glorious dragons with a rainbow of shimmering scales, pride and love filled my chest. Saying goodbye to them and sending them into possible danger was tougher than I expected. Okay, now the tears might come.

My father dashed into the water before I could start crying, preventing me from saying any more sentimental words to my mates. He was probably worried if I stood there any longer, I'd call this whole thing off. I wouldn't, even though the idea was appealing.

The bubble of water surrounded me as Doran swam up toward the light. My mates followed, with Reven and Auric shielding Slade and Jasin. We breached the surface with a huge spray of saltwater, with Doran leaping straight from the ocean to the sky. I heard the others emerge and climb onto the small island, and soon we were all flying high.

At the sight of so many wings catching the wind currents, I longed for my own dragon form too. Soon, I hoped.

We circled each other in one last goodbye, and then everyone took off in separate directions. I watched my mates as their shining bodies got farther and farther away, until I could no longer see them at all.

Doran and I headed south toward the Fire Realm, where he said the elementals had their capital city. I wasn't thrilled to go back to the Fire Realm, which held some bad memories from our encounters with the Onyx Army, but Doran had assured me we wouldn't run into any trouble there.

Over the next few days, Doran soared high in the clouds to avoid anyone catching a glimpse of us and reporting back to the other Dragons. They were still out there somewhere looking for us, and I could only pray that my mates were staying out of sight as well.

When we weren't flying, Doran spent a lot of time training me to use my magic, especially water and earth since I'd had little chance to use them yet. I had the easiest time learning water, which Doran said was due to his blood running through my veins. I wasn't sure if that was true, or if I'd just gotten better at magic overall after using three other elements already.

While we ate, Doran told me stories about his childhood and his life as a pirate, alternating between making me hang onto his every word as he spun a thrilling tale and laughing as he recounted some trouble he'd gotten himself into. I especially liked his stories of his sister Kira, and I could tell they'd been very close all those years ago. But he hardly spoke of anything after he'd been chosen by the Water God and said little about his time with Nysa and the other Dragons. I couldn't tell if the memories were too painful, or if he was purposefully hiding things from me about them.

He asked me a lot of questions about my own past too, although he already knew a lot about it. He'd watched my entire life from the shadows, including during my childhood in the Water Realm, my time with the merchants and the bandits, and when I'd lived in Stoneham for the last few years.

"I saw you once," I said, one night over supper. "When I was fourteen."

"Ah, yes. I was making sure those merchants were looking after you."

"And if they weren't?"

He shrugged. "I would have found a new place for you."

"When I saw you, I was terrified. The only Dragon I'd seen until then had been Sark, and I worried you were looking for me so you could finish his job. I ran away the next morning."

"Yes, I remember. It took me some time to track you down again." He sounded almost...proud. But his response only made me angry.

"For the next few years I was on the run, all alone and living in fear, struggling to find my next meal. Why didn't you help me at any time?"

"I wanted to, many times. All parents want easy lives for their children. If things were different, I'd have made sure you were raised in a palace, with everything you could have ever desired, but I knew that would harm you in the end. An easy life wouldn't have prepared you for what you're going through now. You had to learn to be a survivor and a fighter on your own. So I stayed back and let you find your own way, even though it was torture for me."

I sighed. "I understand, but I can't help but wish I'd known you all my life. Even if I didn't know you were my father, it would have been nice to know someone was on my side."

"It was too dangerous. I couldn't risk Nysa or the other Dragons finding you." He reached over and patted my hand. "I wish things could have been different, but I'm happy I get to spend this time with you now."

He didn't say it, but I knew underneath those words was

the sentiment that our time together would be short. My throat closed up and I had to look away before I started crying. I was starting to wish he would betray us—otherwise there was no way I'd be able to defeat him when the time came.

And if I didn't? Then Nysa would win.

KIRA

When I spotted Valefire, the volcano where the Fire Temple was located, Doran said we were getting close. He continued past it, out over the ocean, toward an island he'd claimed few knew about. Except him, of course.

Hours later, a wide expanse of bright green land came into view in front of us. Mountains stretched high into the sky and smoke rose from one of them. But as we approached, we heard something behind us. The snap of wings.

Doran spun around, his fangs bared, preparing to fight—except when the sunlight caught the other dragon's scales, we saw they were nearly the same shade as Doran's.

"Reven!" I called out, both excited and relieved to see him.

"What's he doing here?" Doran growled, though I

couldn't tell if he was annoyed or not due to his dragon voice.

Reven hovered beside us, looking glorious as a dragon. "I finished my discussions with the Assassin's Guild early and decided to join you here. They said yes, by the way. For a price."

"That's good," I said. "We'll find a way to pay their fee, somehow."

"You didn't trust me with Kira, did you?" Doran asked Reven, his eyes narrowed.

"Of course not," Reven said. "And this way, I can take her into the elemental city instead of you."

He huffed. "You think you can do a better job convincing them than I can?"

Reven stared him down. "Neither one of us is doing that, but Kira will be a lot more convincing if she isn't seen working with the enemy."

"He's right," I said. "Arriving with you was always going to be a problem. It would be better if you waited back by Valefire while Reven and I spoke to the elementals alone."

Doran bared his fangs and I could tell he didn't like this idea, but finally he relented. "Fine. But if you're not back within a day, I'm coming to get you."

"That's acceptable," I said.

The two dark blue dragons landed on the water, folding their legs under them and bobbing up and down on the waves. I carefully switched from Doran's back to Reven's, and then reached out to touch my father's snout.

"We'll meet up with you soon," I said.

Doran grumbled, but then wished me luck before taking off. I leaned forward and wrapped my arms around Reven, pressing my face against his sun-warmed scales.

"I'm so happy to see you again," I said.

"I love you too," he replied. I laughed as he launched into the air.

The island where the elementals lived was huge, but Doran had already told me where we needed to go, and I directed Reven toward the northern end. Crystal clear waters surrounded the island, which was covered in thick green plants everywhere except at the center, where a volcano that rivaled Valefire spewed heat and ash into the sky. We passed it by, flying high overhead, and spotted various structures made of stone dotted across the land.

As we approached the northern end of the island, we spotted more structures below us, forming a large city. Reven swept down toward it, and we began to make out elementals of every kind moving about the streets. Heavy rock elementals trudged alongside floating air elementals, while scorching hot fire elementals spoke with ones made of ice. I'd never seen so many in one place before and had never seen the different types interacting together. I'd always thought elementals stuck to their own kind, and that was that. Clearly I had a lot to learn about them.

Reven swept down and landed at the edge of the city to not cause a panic, but we drew attention anyway. Dozens of elementals surrounded us, their glowing eyes menacing, and I held up my hands in surrender.

"Please don't attack," I called out. "We come in peace and only wish to talk."

"Dragons," a water elemental hissed. "You are not welcome here."

I climbed off of Reven's back and he shifted into his human form. "I know the other Dragons are your enemies, but we are not them. We are the ascendants, and we want to stop the Black Dragon and bring an end to her reign."

"Impossible," an earth elemental grumbled.

"All we ask is that we have a few minutes to speak to your leaders."

The elementals began to speak in their own language of sounds I didn't understand. I heard a crackling, a splash, a gust, and the scraping of stone, and though it seemed they were arguing with each other, it was hard to tell for sure.

"Come with us," a fire elemental finally said, allowing me to breathe again.

A few of the elementals began to lead us inside the city, toward a tall pyramid that reflected sunlight. Made of glass, I realized, as we drew closer. The stone buildings around us were not especially intricate, but they were sturdy and functional. Humans thought elementals were little more than animals, living in caves and attacking cities for resources, but this confirmed my belief they were more like us than people knew.

We were brought inside the pyramid into a large room where four statues of the Gods in their dragon forms stood over their elements. I spotted a fire slowly burning in a pit of coals, a serene pool of water, a garden with fresh dirt, and an altar with incense and wind chimes that released a light tinkling sound. A large chair sat in front of each statue, facing toward the center of the room.

"Wait here," a fire elemental said.

Everyone else left the room then, taking much of the light with them as heavy doors closed and trapped us inside. One beam of light stretched down the top of the pyramid from high above us, dimly illuminating the room from the center.

Another door opened and four elementals entered, each with a small silver circlet on their heads. They took the chairs in front of their God's statues, while Reven and I stood in the center, under the beam of light. Each elemental's glowing eyes pinned us with a stare, though it was difficult to read the emotions on their faces. I tried not to squirm under their gaze, standing tall and facing them with as much confidence as I could muster.

"Spirit Dragon and Water Dragon," the air elemental said. It looked like a barely-contained whirling tornado with arms. "Why are you here?"

"We've come to discuss an alliance," I said.

The fire elemental leaned back in its chair, its body made entirely of flames and radiating heat. "Why would we want such a thing?"

"Because you want the same things we do—to rid of the world of the current Dragons and restore peace between humans and elementals."

"We tried peace before," the water elemental said, with

the body of an upside-down tear that shifted like waves. "In your grandmother's time. It didn't work."

"That was a long time ago, and it might have worked if not for the shades and the Black Dragon. I think it's time we tried again. Or at the very least, let us unite against our common enemies for a short time." I stepped forward and glanced between each of them, putting my heart into my words and hoping they heard my sincerity. "Humans and elementals do not have to be enemies. We're more alike than anyone realizes, and we can learn so much from each other. When I become the next Spirit Dragon, I will be an advocate for both humans *and* elementals. I only want peace and balance—that's the task the Gods have given me."

"We've heard a tale of how you saved one of my kind," the rock elemental spoke up. Like the one I'd rescued, it resembled a giant boulder more than anything, except it had arms and legs. "We owe you a debt, which is why you were allowed to arrive in Divine Isle unharmed. No other human has been so honored in hundreds of years. But that does not mean we trust you."

"I'd like to hear her proposal," the air elemental said.

"A battle will be held at the Spirit Temple on the day of the Fall Equinox. The goal is for my mates and I to get inside the temple, defeat the current Dragons, and take their place. We're looking for allies to fight with us, as we know the other Dragons will have the support of the shades and much of the Onyx Army."

"An impossible battle," the fire elemental said. "You will all be destroyed."

The water elemental waved a fluid hand at the fire elemental, as if trying to shush it, before turning back to me. "Who will fight by your side?"

"The Resistance," I said. "And soldiers from the Air Realm." Probably.

"The Assassin's Guild has agreed to join us as well," Reven added.

"We're also contacting others who might be willing to assist us." I decided it was better not to mention they were bandits. "But we fear it won't be enough, especially against the shades. Not without the aid of the elementals."

The rock elemental crossed its arms. "What you ask is too much. Many of our kind would perish."

"And how many more will perish if things continue as they are?" Reven asked. "The humans, shades, and Dragons all see your kind as an enemy, something that should be wiped out from the world. By helping us, you will begin to change the minds of humans, and remove the Dragons and the shades from power."

"I don't want to put anyone in danger," I said. "But this is the only way to stop the Dragons for good. The Gods chose me and my mates to do this, but we need your help." I swallowed, then added, "Please. For the good of the world."

The elementals began speaking to each other in their strange language, while Reven and I waited. It was clear they were arguing by the raised voices and frantic gestures, but we didn't understand any of it. The earth elemental's grumble made the floors vibrate like an earthquake, while the fire elemental flared so hot it made us step back. The water elemental whipped its arms about, sending cold droplets across the room, while the air elemental's passionate words made our hair and clothes fly back.

When the elementals calmed, they all fixed their glowing eyes on us again. "We cannot help you," the rock elemental said, its voice low and final.

My heart sank. I'd really thought they would agree to help us. After all, we wanted the same things, or so I'd thought. Without the elementals, I wasn't sure if we would stand a chance.

"We cannot get involved in the affairs of humans," the fire elemental said. "Especially when there is no obvious benefit to our kind."

The water elemental nodded. "If you succeed, we will speak to you of a potential alliance then. If not, then none of this will matter anyway."

"But the outcome of this battle affects all of your kind too!" I said. "You can't stand by and do nothing while the world slips further and further into darkness. This is your chance to help bring back balance and peace, for both humans and elementals alike."

"We have given you our answer," the air elemental said. "It's time for you to leave our lands."

"But—"

Reven took my arm. "Come on, Kira. They've made their decision."

I drew in a shaky breath, trying to accept that I had failed. I wanted to yell at them, beg them to help us, plead with them to reconsider, or whatever it would take, but I knew they wouldn't change their minds. The division between humans and elementals was too strong and too old. I'd been a fool to think I could end hundreds of years of conflict so quickly. I'd hoped they would see that we could change, and that I was different from my mother, but they couldn't.

But I *was* different from her. Even if the elementals wouldn't help us, I wouldn't stop fighting for peace. As long as I survived what was to come.

26

SLADE

Kira should have been back by now.

I stared at the horizon in the direction I imagined she would arrive from on the back of a dark blue dragon. Sometimes I thought I saw something, but it was just a bird. It was always a bird.

Auric clasped a hand over my shoulder. "She'll be okay. Reven is with her."

"We don't know that."

I'd been the first to arrive in Clayridge after we'd all set out on our different tasks. Jasin had arrived a day later, with Auric showing up two days after that. And then...we'd waited.

"I can sense them both through the bond," Auric said. "If they were in danger, we'd know it."

"They should have been here by now." I couldn't keep

the scowl off my face. I didn't like being separated from Kira and not being able to see for myself she was safe.

"Come, the hour grows late, and your mother has prepared another feast for us. Staring at the sky isn't going to bring Kira back any faster." He gestured toward the house behind us, where I'd grown up. Warm, hearty smells drifted out of the open windows, beckoning us inside.

"Fine," I grumbled, as I started to turn away. Except from the corner of my eye I spotted something, which made me pause. Another bird, most likely.

Except it was too big for a bird.

"Wait," I said. "What is that?"

We both watched the black speck in the sky as it grew closer. Definitely not a bird.

"It's Reven!" Auric said.

"How can you tell it's him and not Doran?"

"Reven's scales are a darker blue."

I grunted in response as we watched the dragon fly closer, growing larger with each second. When I saw the two people on his back, I could finally breathe easier. As soon as Reven landed, Kira leaped off his back and rushed toward us. I caught her in my arms and squeezed her close, while Auric hugged her from behind.

"I'm so happy to see you both," she said, as we held her between us.

Auric stroked her hair. "It's been far too long."

"We were getting worried about you," I said, pressing my forehead against hers.

"Sorry, it took us longer than expected due to some bad weather, plus we had to go around Soulspire..."

Jasin ran out of the inn and swept Kira up in his arms and spun her around, while she laughed. They shared a few words, while Doran hopped off Reven's back. The older man gave us all a nod, but his face was tight.

"I'll be at the inn," Doran said. "Meet me there tomorrow for breakfast so we can go over everything and begin your next round of training." He strode off into the dark town after that, without bothering to ask where the inn was.

"What's his problem?" Jasin asked.

Reven changed into his human form and walked toward us. "He's been like that ever since we got to Divine Isle, where the elementals live."

"What happened?" Auric asked.

"It's a long story," Kira said. "Is that food I smell? I'm starving."

I took her arm in mine. "Come inside. My mother has cooked way more food than any of us can eat and would be happy to see you."

As soon as we stepped inside, Brin and Leni jumped to their feet. "Kira!" Brin said. The three women exchanged hugs, and then Brin patted the seat next to her. "Sit down and eat. We must hear about where you've been."

"Not before saying hello to me." My mother rushed forward and grabbed Kira in a tight squeeze. "It's so good to see you again, dear."

"And you, Yena," Kira said, placing a kiss on my mother's cheek. "The food smells wonderful, as usual."

"Now you can sit," my mother said, with a laugh. "Leni, help me bring everything out for our guests."

Leni jumped up and ran to the kitchen, then returned with a giant roasted turkey that Jasin had caught us earlier. I began carving it, while they brought out more food—potatoes, onions, peas, and bread—along with tankards of ale.

While we all dug in, Kira told us about her encounter with the elementals, including the beauty of the island, the grandness of their capital, and the disappointment of their refusal to help.

Jasin clenched his fist tightly around his tankard. "I can't believe they said no. Don't they realize that we want to help them too?"

"They want to stay neutral and see what happens," Auric said. "They probably consider it the safest thing to do for their people."

"Cowards," Jasin muttered.

"It's frustrating, but there's nothing we can do about it," I said. "We'll do the best we can without them."

We took a few minutes to load our plates and eat, before Jasin asked, "What's going on with Doran?"

Kira sighed. "He's been distant and grumpy ever since Reven found us. He's upset we don't trust him and thinks he could have done a better job convincing the elementals to join us. Maybe he's right, I don't know."

"He's not," Reven said. "The elementals hate the other

Dragons. If he'd been with you, they wouldn't have spoken to you at all."

"Perhaps." She drew in a long breath and gazed across the table at me and Auric. "Please tell me the rest of you had better luck."

"We did," Auric said. "My father agreed to send troops from the Air Realm's division of the Onyx Army, along with plenty of supplies. My brother Garet will be leading them."

"Thank the Gods," Kira said, closing her eyes briefly. "And what of the others?"

Jasin took a sip of his ale. "Cadock took a lot of convincing, but he finally agreed in exchange for his people being pardoned of all their crimes and given positions in your new government or military."

Kira raised her eyebrows. "I'm surprised he agreed at all. I'm sure we can figure something out for them."

"The Assassin's Guild has agreed to fight with us as well," Reven told us. "For a fee, naturally."

"That's good news," Auric said.

"The Resistance is willing to help, of course," I said. "Although they have fewer people than they did before due to the fight at Salt Creek Tower. However, they're sending messages to their other bases and expect a lot more people to join. Especially now that rumors have become widespread about a second group of Dragons."

"Is that so?" Kira asked.

"The Resistance have been spreading them," Leni said. "All thanks to Brin."

Brin nodded, a slight smile on her lips. "People need something to fight for, a cause to rally behind. Tales of how you've fought the Dragons are spreading like wildfire. You're already becoming legendary. I expect more people are joining the fight against the Dragons every day."

"Yes, but did you have to go with those names?" Jasin asked, arching a brow. "Ruby Dragon, really?"

Brin laughed. "Trust me, people love them. It sounds regal, like you were meant to rule."

"It could be worse," Leni said. "They could call you the Pink Dragon."

"My scales are not even close to pink!" Jasin said.

"What are they calling me?" Reven asked, as he tore off a piece of bread.

"The Sapphire Dragon," Auric said. "I'm Citrine, and Slade is Emerald."

Reven made a face. "I don't remember agreeing to that."

Leni grinned, clearly enjoying every second of this. "Too bad. The names have spread now, and you're stuck with them."

I began ticking off a list on my fingers. "So we'll have people from the Resistance, the Air Realm's army, the bandits, and the Assassin's Guild. Will it be enough?"

"Oh, and Calla and her priests," Auric added. "They're still in Stormhaven under the protection of my father, but they wanted to help us."

"Good," Kira said. "It will be useful to have another magic user there. Especially against the shades. I don't know if it will be enough, not without the elementals, but it will have to do."

"There's one thing that might help," I said. "While we waited for you, we've been working on imbuing our weapons with magic. I think we've mastered it now, and we can do your sword tomorrow."

"Yes, look at this." Jasin stood up, moved back from the table, and pulled out his sword. The blade lit up on fire, making Kira gasp.

"We did it to all our weapons," Auric explained.

Reven leaned forward, his eyes intrigued. "Can you do my swords too?"

"Yes, I can," I said. "And now that you're here, we can enchant Kira's sword too, with all four elements. We'll get started tomorrow."

"How long do you think you'll be in town?" my mother asked.

"About a week," Kira said.

My mother sighed, but nodded. "Well, I wish it were longer, but I know you have important things to do. It's just so good having all my children back in Clayridge." She wrapped her arm around Leni and gave her a squeeze, before turning back to us with a smile. "And you too, Kira. All of you, really. It's been a delight getting to know Auric and Jasin the last few days, and I'm sure you're just as lovely, Reven. You're all family now."

Reven shifted in his seat, looking uncomfortable, while Kira's cheeks flushed. I reached over to take her hand and gave it a squeeze. I'd once worried my family would never accept our relationship or this situation, but my mother had treated Kira like my betrothed and the other men as if they were my brothers. I knew she worried about us and the upcoming battle, but she believed in us and in our destiny. I couldn't ask for anything more...except that we make it through the battle alive.

We met with my father in the morning to go over everything the others had learned on their journey and to discuss strategy. After that, my mates and I went to Slade's old forge, which was now run by his cousin, Noren.

The blacksmith's shop was open on one side, allowing smoke to billow out. I leaned against a tree as I watched my men work. Slade enchanted Reven's twin swords first, until they gleamed with a thin coat of sharp, deadly ice.

Slade walked over to me. "We're ready for your sword now."

I pulled my blade out of its sheath. Auric had bought it for me early in our adventures, and it was still the nicest thing I owned. It also fit my hand perfectly, the weight and balance exactly suited for my size.

I chewed on my lip as I handed it to him. "You're sure this will work?"

He nodded. "Trust me. I've done this to all of our weapons now."

"Yes, but you only did one element then."

"I'm confident it will work. If not, I'll make you a new sword. I promise."

He returned to the forge, where he heated up the metal in my blade. I squirmed as it turned red-hot, and that's when he placed it on a slab between my four mates. They stood in a circle around it, holding hands with each other, their eyes closed. Nothing happened at first, and I worried all of this was for nothing, but then I felt the magic growing. Fire danced across the sword before sinking into it. A gust of air swirled around it, and the blade absorbed that too, followed by a ripple of water that turned to ice, cooling the sword down. The metal hardened and shifted color, becoming lighter and stronger.

When the men stepped back and opened their eyes, my sword emitted a faint silver glow. Slade picked it up and presented it to me.

"A sword fit for the Silver Dragon," he said.

I wrapped my hand around the hilt and was struck by the powerful magic running through it. All four elements were in there, acting as one. I held the blade up to the sunlight and it flashed bright silver.

Yes, this was a sword that could take down Dragons.

W hile the men practiced using their enchanted weapons against each other, I sat on an old tree trunk and ate some dried fruit. My sword lay across my lap, but I was hesitant to use it against my mates now for fear of truly hurting them.

Doran leaned against a tree beside me, making me jump. I hadn't heard him approach. Sometimes he was a little too much like Reven, sneaking about like that.

"Nice sword," he said. "Can I see it?"

"Of course." I handed it to him before popping a dried apricot in my mouth.

He held it up, testing the weight, catching the light. When he held it, the silvery glow dimmed, as if it only reacted strongly to my magic. He gave a few practice swipes at the air, and then he grunted. "Not bad. Now the real test."

He sliced the blade across his forearm, opening a thick cut. Fire danced across his skin, and the edges of the wound blackened. He let out a sharp hiss and staggered back.

I jumped to my feet and ran to him. "What are you doing?"

"Testing it out, since you won't do it yourself."

"I didn't want to hurt anyone!"

He gave me a sharp look as he pressed a hand over his wound. "I hope that mercy won't hold you back when the time comes."

I rolled my eyes. "Let me see your wound. Maybe I can do something for it."

"I doubt it."

I clasped my hands over the wound, feeling how hot his skin was, while blood slipped through my fingers. "I was able to heal the Fire Priestess."

"Were you?" His eyebrow arched. "Guess it can't hurt to try."

I focused on his wound, trying to stop the bleeding, reaching for the life magic always lingering inside me. It was much harder to send it into my father than it was to heal my mates. He and I didn't have the bond entwining our lives together, but there was something else instead. A recognition that a part of us was the same.

Slowly the bleeding stopped, and the cut sealed itself up. The burn took the longest to heal, as if the fire magic that caused it was fighting me still. But in the end, I won the battle, and his skin was smooth again.

Doran held up his arm and inspected it. "Impressive. I'm not sure even Nysa could heal someone who wasn't one of her mates."

"It only worked because you're my father. The magic sensed that we were connected." I took the sword from him and sheathed it. "Well, did it meet your expectations?"

"It did. I wanted to make sure my water magic wouldn't block it, but that wasn't a problem. Instead it burned me with fire, while air and earth helped make it stronger. Quite painful and potent. It will be able to take down any of the Dragons, including Nysa once she's weakened."

I sank back onto my tree stump, suddenly exhausted from the healing. "Why have you been so distant for the last few days? Ever since we met with the elementals you've been acting oddly."

"I'm sorry. I guess I got upset when Reven arrived and I realized none of you trust me still. I don't care about what the others think, but I thought you and I had become close." He ran a hand through his long, sandy hair. "Or as close as we could be, considering the circumstances."

"I do trust you, but I also knew that Reven was right and we had a better chance of getting the elementals to help us without you there." I sighed. "Not that it made much difference in the end."

His hand rested on my shoulder. "You did the best you could. The elementals were never going to help us."

"I realize that now. I just don't know how to defeat the Dragons without them."

"Hmm." He glanced up at the sky. "It won't be easy. Especially since the Dragons know we're here now and have probably guessed our plans."

I sat up straight, my muscles tensing. "They do?"

"I've felt both Sark and Heldor's presence nearby."

"Will they attack Clayridge?"

"No, they'd have to be stupid to do that. We outnumber them, and you can control all the elements now. They're just watching and waiting to see what we do next."

I chewed on my lower lip, worrying about the innocent lives in this village. Doran couldn't know for sure that the Dragons wouldn't attack. "Maybe we should leave soon."

"Wherever we go, we'll put people at risk. That's why

we have to face them soon. Only problem is, they know we're coming. They'll be preparing too."

My fists clenched. "So be it. As you said, this has to end soon. One way or another."

Doran's eyes caught mine, mirroring my own. "Just remember, you're my daughter. Whatever happens, I'm on your side. Always."

I swallowed the unexpected emotions rising inside me. "I know, father."

28

AURIC

"Today we're going to work on combining the elements," Doran said. It was time for yet another training session, and we all stood beside the river and faced him, with the afternoon sun bright in the sky. "I already know you can do lightning, thanks to Kira hitting me with a bolt when I was rescuing her."

Kira shrugged. "I thought you were taking me to my death."

Doran snorted. "How did you learn to do that one anyway?"

"Enva told us it was possible and then it was a lot of trial and error," I said.

"And frustration," Jasin added. "Mostly frustration."

Doran scratched at his scraggly beard. "You've done well, considering you had no one to train you. What other combinations can you do?"

"That's it so far," Kira said. "The bond with Slade and Reven was too new to do any others yet."

Doran nodded. "Hopefully it's grown enough by now. The benefit of combining elements is that there's no immunity to them. Both Sark and Isen can be hurt by lightning, for example."

"What will we do about Nysa?" Reven asked. "She's immune to every element."

"You let me worry about her," Doran said. "After the other dragons are defeated, she'll be vulnerable to attack."

I thought about asking whether that included him, but the troubled look on Kira's face made me hold my tongue.

"The hardest elements to combine are the two opposite ones," Doran continued. "Fire and water make steam, while earth and air create sandstorms. We'll work our way up to those. You can already do lightning, so we'll skip that."

"We want to learn to make lava," Slade said. "Or at least be able to stop it."

"A good choice. Probably the most deadly and destructive of the combined elements. Fine, you two can work together today, while Auric and Reven will make fog."

"Fog?" Jasin asked. "How will that be useful?"

Doran crossed his arms. "Not everything is about striking your enemies down. Sometimes there are better ways of handling things. Fog can conceal and confuse. It can hide a huge group of soldiers on the battlefield. It can make it easier to escape from a bad situation. And when you get good enough, you can make clouds and cover the sky with them too."

"It sounds perfect," I said, thinking of all the possibilities. With both Reven and Jasin's magic flowing through me, I could create entire storms on my own.

Reven and I moved closer to the forest, while Jasin and Slade headed for the edge of the river in case they had problems. But as I faced Reven, I began to have doubts this would work. I didn't know him all that well yet, and his bond with Kira was new. Jasin and I had become close, despite our differences, and Slade and I had an easy understanding and friendship. But Reven? He was hard for all of us to get to know. Kira had often commented on how Reven pushed her away or locked her out, but it wasn't only her that he kept at a distance. Combining our magic took a connection, and the man was a wall of ice that was nearly impossible to cross. Luckily, I knew how to fly.

"Fog would have been useful in your previous profession, I imagine," I said.

Reven let out a soft grunt in response. "Those days are over."

"Yes. I wanted to thank you again for what you did for my father. You didn't have to do that." Reven had taken the contract on my father's life to make sure no one else did, even though it ended his career with the Assassin's Guild forever.

"I wasn't going to kill him," Reven said, sending me a sharp look.

"No, of course not." Damn, I was really bungling this one up. "I simply meant that I appreciated how you handled it, and the sacrifice it required of you."

"It was time to move on from that life anyway."

"And yet you went back to them to ask for their help. Was it a problem, since you failed to complete your last mission?"

He smirked. "It was, until I turned into a dragon in front of them and made it rain in the middle of the room."

I grinned back at him. "I would have loved to have seen their faces."

"All right," Doran called out, interrupting us. "Try to reach for your partner's magic through the bond. It might be difficult to find at first, but it's there. Once you've found it, grab tight and let it loose with your own magic."

I stared into Reven's cold blue eyes, searching for him within the bond. Jasin was easy to find, like a bright spark jumping behind my eyes that grew stronger with my attention on him. Slade was harder to find, but when I focused on him, his steady, strong presence filled my mind. Creating a storm of sand or dust with him wouldn't be too difficult, I imagined. But when I searched for Reven, I felt nothing.

"This isn't working," Reven said.

"It will. It took a long time for me and Jasin to figure it out, but we did eventually."

"The two of you are close," Reven said, his lip curling as if the idea bothered him. "But you and me? We have nothing in common."

"I don't think that's true." I tilted my head, studying him. "Jasin and Slade both let their emotions dominate them. With Jasin it's obvious, but Slade is just as guilty of it, he just doesn't react as passionately or as hastily. His emotions build up under the surface, until they can't be contained anymore. But you and I—we think things through. We take our time. We research different options before we come to a decision. We both value knowledge above most other things. Our lives have been completely different, but we're more alike than you think."

"I suppose," Reven said. "Although you value knowledge for the sake of having it. I value what it can do for me. It's a means to an end, not an end in and of itself."

"True, but we still prefer to trust our minds more than our hearts, which can make it difficult for us to open up to people or can lead us to make bad decisions. I made mistakes with Kira that I now regret. I kept secrets from her about who I was, because my mind told me it was the best thing to do at the time. Maybe if I'd listened to my heart, things would have been easier."

Reven was silent, staring at the river's flowing water. Behind us, Jasin let out a shout as he and Slade made the ground rip apart and lava shoot from the cracks, while Kira and Doran applauded.

"Maybe you're right," Reven finally said. "I locked away my heart for so many years I'd convinced myself I didn't have one anymore. Kira forced me to realize I was wrong about that."

I chuckled softly. "She has a way of making us confront the things about ourselves we would like to ignore. Annoying, isn't it?"

"Very." Reven let out a long breath. He glanced over at Jasin and Slade, the star pupils of today's training session, as they made lava spurt into the air. "We can't let them show us up. How do we do this?"

"Jasin and I found it easier if we were holding hands and staring into each other's eyes. Maybe that would help?" I stretched out my hands toward him, palms up.

Reven rolled his eyes and grabbed my hands. "Fine."

His skin was cool against mine, and his eyes were the pale blue of the early morning sky. When I searched for him through the bond this time, I found a small, cold ripple. I grasped onto it, pulling it toward me, unwilling to let go, and the ripple became a wave, growing stronger the more I tugged at it. Now that I knew what he felt like in my mind, I was certain I could find him again, and it would be easier next time.

When Reven's breathing suddenly changed and his eyes widened, I knew he'd found me through the bond too. His fingers tightened around mine and something passed between us. The air around us began to grow murky. Fog rolled off the water, creeping around the forest, becoming thicker with each passing second. Soon, I couldn't see anything except Reven. The rest of the world had been cut off, hidden away by the magic we'd created. I saw the wonder in his eyes as he took it in, and then we grinned at each other. Somehow, I didn't think we'd have a problem connecting anymore.

29

KIRA

Over the next week we trained harder than we ever
had before. We faced each other in teams and one
on one. We fought with our weapons, with our magic alone,
or—for the men—in their dragon forms. Doran barked out
orders the entire time, pushing us to fight harder, to keep
going, to never back down. He gave us tips on the other
Dragons' weaknesses and showed us how to use our powers
together to defeat them. We learned more from him than we
had in the entire few months we'd known each other.

And I worried it still wouldn't be enough.

Every night, we returned to our rooms in the inn,
exhausted, beaten, bloody, and burnt. My men and I had no
energy for lovemaking—we simply curled up in bed
together, all five of us holding each other tenderly, and my
touch healed my mates while we slept. Our bonds grew
stronger, and with it, our magic.

The other Dragons had hundreds of years on us. We would never be as strong or as experienced as them. But we had something they'd lost over the years—love.

The days rushed by, and soon it was time for another bittersweet goodbye as we said farewell to Slade's family and the town that had sheltered us not once, but twice. We packed our things, hugged everyone tightly, and then prepared to take off—and that's when I noticed we were one person short.

"Where's Doran?" I asked, as I glanced about.

Slade frowned. "It's not like him to run late."

"I saw him fly away last night," Leni said. "I assumed you knew, so I didn't mention it."

I took a step back as my knees nearly gave out on me. The world spun around me, and I felt like I might actually throw up. "He left?"

"Oh Gods," Auric said, his eyes wide. "Doran had the map with all the battle plans. If he took that with him..."

Jasin swore under his breath. "That bastard. I knew he'd betray us!"

"We don't know that for certain," Brin said, though her voice wasn't very convincing. She rested a sympathetic hand on my back. "There must be some explanation."

"Yes, exactly." I clung to her words, desperate to hold onto hope. I refused to believe my father would betray us, after everything he'd done. "He told me to remember he's on my side. Maybe he's not really betraying us but trying to help us in some way."

Slade wrapped a strong arm around me. "I know you

want to believe that, but it doesn't seem likely. If he was helping us, he would have told us his plan, not sneak off in the middle off the night."

"The Water God warned us about this," Reven said. "He said Doran would turn against us because he would never be willing to give up the power and his own life."

"But why would he help us all this time only to betray us?" I asked.

"Because he wanted us to trust him!" Jasin growled. "Now he's run back to Nysa and he knows all our weaknesses and our plans."

"We'll have to completely redo our strategy," Auric said, his brow furrowed. "If that is even possible."

Jasin's eyes flashed with anger. "We can adjust some things, but he'll be able to anticipate which ones. We're doomed. We might as well call this all off now."

"We can't call it off," Brin said. "We'll just have to do the best we can."

I stared at my mates, feeling their rage and frustration through the bond, and knew they were right. My father really had betrayed us. Everything he'd told me was a lie. All this time he'd been working for Nysa, acting as her scout and her spy, like he always did. And we'd played right into his hand, doing everything he asked, falling for all of his lies. In the end, he was as corrupted as she was, and there was no redemption for him.

I clenched my hand around my sword, feeling the magic within it. "We're going to continue with our plans. And when we come face to face with the Dragons, we'll destroy them." My voice hardened into steel. "All of them."

We set off for the Spirit Temple, which was in the middle of a large plain just south of Soulspire. We'd advised all our allies to meet us in a valley east of there on the day of the Fall Equinox. It would take us a few days to get there, and it never escaped my mind that Doran was hours ahead of us with all of our plans. My mates pushed themselves hard, flying as fast and as long as they could, and every night they were completely exhausted.

On the last night before we expected to arrive, I tossed and turned beside my men, unable to sleep. All I could think about was facing my father, and what I would have to do to stop him. Eventually I stood and walked away, hoping the quiet forest would bring me some peace.

I found Enva sitting on a large rock nearby, like she'd been waiting for me for hours.

"Hello, Kira. Come sit beside me."

I leaned against the stone, gazing across the dark forest and listening to the quiet sounds of night. "Did Doran really betray us?"

"It seems that way. He's heading to Soulspire now with your battle plans. I'm sorry."

I covered my face with my hands as I tried to gain control over my emotions. "I can't trust my mother. I can't trust my father. I'm not even sure I can trust you. The only people I can count on are my mates."

"Yes, as it should be." She patted my arm softly. "Doran had to return to Nysa. He is bound by magic to be loyal to her. He might have been able to resist it for some time, but when she calls him through the bond, it's difficult to ignore."

"Does he even care for me at all?"

"Yes, I'm sure he does. He did save your life as a baby, and he has watched over you your whole life, much as I have. But he has been bound to Nysa for nearly a thousand years. Their lives are entwined. It's difficult for him to fight against her, even for you."

"I feel so stupid. Everyone warned me not to trust him, but I wanted to believe in him."

"You're not stupid. You wanted a father. There is nothing wrong with that."

"There is when he now has all of your secrets and can turn them against you."

"Don't give up hope." She smoothed my head softly, the touch so nurturing it surprised me. "You and your mates were chosen by the Gods to protect this world. I have faith that you'll succeed."

I leaned against her body, which looked frail but was surprisingly sturdy, especially considering she was a ghost. "I wish I didn't have to kill my parents," I whispered, giving voice to the thing I'd kept inside so long and was afraid to admit.

"I know. I wish the same thing." She sighed and continued stroking my hair. "It's a terrible situation the

Gods have placed us in, but there's no other way. If it makes you feel better, I believe by ending my daughter's life, you will be freeing her. She wasn't always like this. She was brave, and kind, and passionate. Sometimes a little too confident, arrogant, and reckless, but she took after her father, my Fire Dragon. Like him, she would do anything to protect other people, which is why she imprisoned the Spirit Goddess inside herself. Now she's become corrupted and I don't recognize her anymore, but I know my daughter is in there somewhere, screaming for all of this to end." She took my face in her hands gently. "Deep down, Nysa wants you to win too. I truly believe this."

I nodded slowly and she wiped away a stray tear I couldn't hold back. "I'll do my best to free her."

She wrapped her arms around me. "I know you will. You're the only one who can."

With those words, she vanished.

I sat there for some time, listening to the sounds of forest, thinking about Enva's words. I didn't know if she was right about my parents or not. The more I learned about myself and the world, the less I truly knew for certain. All I could do was listen to my gut and hope it led me down the right path in the days to come.

A branch snapped behind me, and I sensed Jasin approaching. His strong arms slid around me, and I relaxed against him. He said nothing, simply held me close, letting me draw upon his strength until I was ready to talk.

"Now I know how you felt when your father betrayed us," I said.

"It's a terrible feeling, isn't it?" He pressed a kiss to the top of my head. "It's horrible enough when your parents believe in something you know is wrong, and no matter how much you try to convince them otherwise, they won't be persuaded to see your side. When they turn against you for those same beliefs, it's like a dagger in the heart."

I leaned my head against his shoulder. "You were right about Doran all along. I should have listened to you."

"I wish I'd been wrong. Gods know I'd do anything to save you from going through this and from suffering the same hurt that I did." He smoothed my hair away from my face and gazed into my eyes. "But we're not defined by what our parents do. We make our own choices, and we can choose to make better decisions than them. Or we can try, at least."

I turned in his arms and pressed a kiss to his lips. "When did you become so wise?"

"I'm spending too much time with Auric obviously."

I snuggled up against him. "I like that the two of you are close."

"We're a family, all five of us—thanks to you. You brought us together, and you made us work out our differences and fight for a common goal. You made each of us want to be better people. And no matter what happens, none of us will ever betray each other. Or you."

The truth of his words flowed through our bond. My adopted parents were long gone, my birth parents were my enemies, but my mates...they were forever.

30

KIRA

As my dragons soared over the peaks of the mountains, the valley beyond it came into view, and with it, our army. It was the day of the Fall Equinox, and hundreds of men and women had come to fight for our cause. I was honored by their bravery and their belief in us, but also felt the heavy weight of their lives hanging over my head. I was responsible for all of them and would mourn every life lost in my name.

On the eastern side, Onyx Army soldiers were assembled, their scaled black armor decorated with the yellow markings on their shoulders that meant they were from the Air Realm. Mixed in with them were others in golden armor with the symbol of House Killian on their chest, representing the royal guard. The King had truly come through for us, and by sending his troops he was showing the world he stood with us against the Dragons. If we failed today, it would likely mean the end of his reign.

To the west, a more ragtag group of men and women had gathered, which I assumed was a combination of the Resistance, the Assassin's Guild, and Cadock's people. They wore common clothes and whatever armor and weapons they possessed. Some were bandits. Some were farmers. Some were assassins. Many were seasoned fighters, but many more were not. Yet they were all here, willing to fight for what they believed in. I prayed we weren't sending them all to their deaths.

In the center, large tents had been set up, and that's where we headed. Faces looked up at us and cheered or simply stared in awe as my four dragons flew overhead. As we descended, I heard shouts about the ascendants and cheers for the Ruby, Sapphire, Emerald, and Citrine Dragons. The men might not love the names, but as Brin had said, they'd already stuck.

People backed away as my dragons landed, giving us space. I slid off Slade's back and nodded at everyone. I wasn't used to so much attention and didn't particularly like it, but I had to get used to this sort of reception. I'd spent so much of my life hiding and running, sticking to the shadows and avoiding being noticed, but those days were over. Everything had changed now, and soon the entire world would know who I was, no matter the outcome of this battle.

While Brin and Leni dismounted, a man in gold armor stalked toward us. I immediately recognized him as one of Auric's brothers, even though we'd never met before. He was ridiculously tall, even taller than Auric, and wasn't lacking in muscles either, judging by the way he filled out his armor. But where Auric's face was chiseled perfection, this man was plain, with blond hair cropped short, pale gray eyes, and a square jaw.

My dragons shifted to their human forms, sending a ripple of awe through the crowd, and Auric stepped forward. The two blond men clasped each other in a hug.

"Thanks for coming." He turned toward me with a smile. "Kira, this is my brother, Garet. He leads the King's Guard."

"A pleasure, my lady," Garet said, with an elegant bow.

"It's nice to meet you," I said.

"Garet will be leading my father's troops," Auric said.

His brother nodded. "Yes, we have men and women from both the King's Guard and the Air Realm's Onyx Army division. We're ready to serve however we can."

"We appreciate your help," I said.

Brin moved to our side with a smile. "It's good to see you again, Garet."

The three nobles continued chatting, but my attention was drawn to another man approaching us. I walked toward him with a smile I couldn't hide. "Cadock!"

The man I'd once considered my first love grasped me in a friendly hug before stepping back. He looked down at me with his bright blue eyes, while his tousled blond hair blew in the breeze. "You're looking as beautiful as ever."

I smiled but ignored the compliment. "I'm so happy you changed your mind about helping us."

"I didn't want to, but your man here is pretty persuasive," Cadock said, nodding at Jasin, who'd come to stand beside us.

Jasin shook Cadock's hand with a wry grin. "I did what I had to do."

"How did you convince him in the end?" I asked. "I never got the whole story."

Cadock smirked. "Jasin challenged me to a fight. If he won, I had to agree to support your cause."

"And if you won?" I asked.

"He'd have to clean our outhouse for a week."

"Don't worry, there was no chance I was going to lose," Jasin said.

Cadock chuckled. "So you say, but as I recall it came pretty close there at the end."

I shook my head as they continued to joke around, and spotted Faya speaking to some people, including Slade's sister, at the edge of the crowd. I made my way over to her with a frown. "You shouldn't be here."

"Hello, Kira," Faya said. "Of course I should be here. I'm the leader of the Resistance now."

"You're also pregnant," I said.

"Only a few months," Faya said, waving it away. "I'll stay back during the fight, but I'm not going to send my people into battle without me. What kind of leader would I be?"

"And if the fighting reaches you?" I asked.

"I'll be fine." Faya touched the hilt of her sword. "I can

still fight. And now I have another thing worth dying for —my child."

Leni moved to Faya's side. "Don't worry. Brin and I will protect her with our lives."

"I appreciate that," I said.

"I don't need protection," Faya snapped, but then she sighed. "But I wouldn't mind having two friends fight beside me."

Cadock and Jasin strolled over. The bandit leader bowed before Faya, then took her hand and placed a kiss over her knuckles. "Why hello there. I'm Cadock, leader of the Thunder Chasers. You must be Faya. I've heard a great deal about you, but no one ever mentioned your beauty."

Faya rolled her eyes. "Probably because they knew I'd cut them in half for speaking about me that way."

A charming smile spread across Cadock's face. "Beautiful and fierce. I love it."

Reven caught my attention, bringing over an older woman with short, white hair and a tattoo of a dagger on her neck. She was dressed in all black, with a hooded cloak that didn't conceal the numerous throwing knives at her waist. "Kira, this is Zara. She'll be speaking for the Assassin's Guild. She also helped train me when I first joined."

"Is that so?" My eyebrows shot up. This was the first person I'd ever met from Reven's past. "What was he like back then?"

Zara grinned. "Just as surly and brooding as he is now. A fine fighter though. I knew the moment we met that he was meant for something big. I had no idea it would be this though."

"None of us expected anything like this," I said. "We appreciate the help of the Assassin's Guild."

She shrugged. "We go where the coin is. And we've been promised a lot of it."

"You'll definitely be compensated," I said. Assuming we made it through this alive.

Zara slapped Reven on the back. "We protect our own too. Reven is one of us, and now he's a Dragon. We'll do whatever we can to assist him."

Reven looked surprised by this. "Thank you, Zara."

"Don't get too soppy on me," Zara said with a grin. "We're mostly here for the coin."

"Of course," I said.

Another familiar face emerged from the crowd. Calla, the High Priestess of the Fire God. She was a beautiful woman in her forties, with hair the color of straw, and she wore the red silk robe of her station. She started to bow before me, but I grabbed her in a hug instead.

"I'm so happy you're okay," I said. "Many of the other priests have been killed by the Dragons."

"So I've heard," Calla said, as she stepped back. "The Air Realm has been kind to us, although I do miss our home at the volcano. I pray we'll be able to return to the Fire Temple once this is all over."

"I hope so." I chewed on my lower lip. "Although we've discovered everything is more complicated than we expected."

I quickly told her about the Spirit Goddess and Nysa, hoping she had some advice for how to stop her.

"I've never heard of such a thing," Calla said. "But if anyone can stop her, it is you."

"Do you think the Gods will truly help us?"

"I cannot say. Sometimes the things they do seem confusing to us, but later on they make sense. They see a much larger picture than we do." She touched my cheek. "Have faith, Kira. You were destined for this, and you will succeed."

Jasin raised his voice, drawing our attention. "If you'd all head inside the tent, we can get started working on our strategy for tomorrow's battle."

I drew in a steady breath as the gathered people stepped into the large command tent to begin preparations. Jasin and Auric had made some changes to our plan after Doran left, but they wanted to get the input of the other leaders too. I watched them all filter in through the tent flaps, and then I followed them inside.

31

KIRA

We spent hours going over every single detail of tomorrow's battle, hammering out the plans until everyone was satisfied with them. Or as satisfied as we could be, considering tomorrow we'd be going up against a far more powerful opponent and many people would die in the battle. Worry gnawed at me, not just for the people I loved, but for everyone who would be fighting for us tomorrow. I wished there was some way to spare them all from this, but to save the world we had to go to war.

The hour was late and the camp was quiet by the time we retreated to the tent that had been set up for us. Originally, we'd been given five tents, but I'd asked for one large tent instead. This might be our last night in this world, and I was going to spend it with my mates at my side.

Five cots had been set up around the room, but we

shoved them to the side and then covered the floor with blankets and pillows. We spread out on the makeshift bed, facing each other like we'd done beside so many campfires during our travels. Now our journey was almost at an end, and the feeling was bittersweet. Especially since we had no idea what the outcome would be tomorrow.

Slade's large hands settled on my shoulders and he began massaging them slowly. "You seem tense."

I leaned back into his touch. "Just worried about tomorrow."

"We all are," Auric said. "But we've done everything we can to make sure the battle goes our way. Now we just need to get some rest."

Jasin rested his hand on my thigh. "We will, but not yet."

"What are you planning?" I asked.

He brushed his lips against my neck. "We're going to take your mind off tomorrow."

I relaxed a little more and tilted my head to give him better access. "All I want is to spend the evening in the arms of my mates...in case it's our last time together."

"Don't talk like that," Slade said, his fingers tightening on my shoulders.

Reven took my face in his hands. "Tomorrow is not going to be the end, I promise."

Jasin nodded. "Our close bond gives us an advantage. The other Dragons don't stand a chance."

Through the bond I knew they were worried too, but

they were also confident we'd succeed. I focused on that certainty and nodded.

Auric began removing my boots. "You definitely need to release some tension. Otherwise you'll never get to sleep."

Jasin's lips traced patterns on my neck. "I know the best way to do that."

While Auric began rubbing my feet, the other three men slowly removed my clothes, lightly kissing every spot of skin they revealed. I melted into their gentle, comforting touches, and by the time I was undressed, I was little more than a puddle in their arms.

"We're going to take care of you," Slade said, as he lowered me down onto my back. "Just relax and enjoy it."

From the pile of blankets and pillows I stared up at the tent while the four men surrounded me. Auric kissed his way up from my ankles to my knees to my thighs, while the others kissed the sensitive skin at the inside of my arms, the curve of my breasts, and the slope of my stomach. Their love wrapped around me like a warm blanket, easing all of my troubles.

Auric spread my legs wider and dipped his head between them, kissing me there. As his mouth moved over me and his tongue began to explore, the others continued their slow worship of the rest of my body. I reached for them, grabbing onto their shirts and trousers, wishing I could touch them too. My fingers brushed against the hard bulge in Reven's trousers and the rough beard coating Slade's jaw, while Jasin's lips found mine.

As Auric wound me tighter and tighter with the stroke of his tongue between my legs, my other mates removed their clothing. The sight of their strong bodies being slowly revealed made me almost dizzy with desire, and I tangled my hands in Auric's golden hair as the tension built inside me. He increased the pressure of his tongue and it became too much, making me gasp and moan as the orgasm gripped me.

Auric sat back and removed his clothing next, while I floated down from the place he'd taken me. My four mates gazed at me with lust-filled eyes and I couldn't decide which one I wanted first.

"I need you," I told them. "All of you. Don't hold back."

Jasin removed a small bottle of oil from one of his bags. "We won't. We're all going to be yours tonight."

My pulse sped up at his words and at what the oil meant. We'd used it once before, and I was excited to try it again with all my men. "Two at a time?" I asked, my voice practically begging.

"If that's what you want," Reven said.

"I do. Auric and Slade. Reven and Jasin. The opposite elements inside me at the same time."

"That can be arranged," Slade said.

I'd been worried he wouldn't be interested in sharing me like that, but he didn't even hesitate as he pulled me toward him and began kissing me, his hard, naked body pressing against my soft curves. Auric's hands fell on my behind, giving it a squeeze.

ELIZABETH BRIGGS

"I've always wanted to take you here," Auric said, sliding his finger between my cheeks. "Ever since I saw Jasin do it."

"Please," I said, before Slade's mouth claimed mine again.

Jasin poured some oil on his hand and began to rub it against my tight entrance, while Auric laid back on the blankets and coated his cock, getting it nice and slippery. Jasin's fingers slid into me easily, stretching me and preparing me for Auric, and then he moved aside.

Slade's hands circled my waist, and he guided me backwards onto Auric, so I straddled him in reverse. Auric gripped my hips, and together the two of them guided me down. I felt Auric's hard length at my back entrance and tensed for a moment, but then my body relaxed as I slowly sank down onto him. I groaned as my tight hole stretched against his large size, and Slade wrapped his arms around me to hold me in place.

"Are you okay?" he asked.

I nodded and lowered myself even more, taking Auric inside me inch by inch. With every second that passed the uncomfortable stretching gave way to pleasure as he filled me up, until my behind rested against his hips and he was completely inside me.

"Gods, you're so tight, Kira," Auric said from behind me, his voice strained almost like he was in pain. "It's incredible."

"You feel so big," I said, rocking a little against him.

"Ready for me too?" Slade asked, his brow furrowed like he worried he might hurt me.

I slid a hand around his neck and drew him toward me

198

to kiss him, my need for him growing with every second. "Very ready."

Auric held my hips while Slade got in position in front of me. His large cock edged into me, and it seemed impossible they would both fit, but somehow Slade pushed all the way inside. I wrapped my arms around his neck as my body grew weak, already overcome with pleasure from being taken by both of them at once.

Slade held me tight, steadying me, as he started to slide in and out. With every thrust he pushed me back onto Auric, and every time he retreated, Auric lifted his hips to follow. I threw my head back and let their rhythmic glide rock me between them, their movements almost leisurely, like they could do this all night. Their long, deep thrusts touched me everywhere, filling me completely. I found myself matching their speed and then increasing it, demanding more from them as I spiraled higher and higher, chasing the release only they could bring. We reached it together, shaking and moaning as the bond snapped tight between us.

I slowly came back down to earth while Slade kissed me and Auric's hands caressed my back and hips. On either side of us, Reven and Jasin watched, stroking themselves as they waited for their turn with me.

Slade kissed me one last time, before he stood and helped lift me off Auric. My knees were so weak I could barely stand, but Jasin was immediately there, sweeping me into his arms. He wrapped my legs around his waist, and I clung to his neck as our lips found each other's. He devoured my mouth as his cock plunged inside me, making me cry out.

Reven moved to stand behind us and his hands cupped my bottom. He'd already oiled himself, and he pushed into my back entrance, pinning me between him and Jasin. I was stretched wide thanks to Auric and Slade, and both Reven and Jasin filled me easily.

Together they held me up as they caged me between their hard bodies and began to thrust into me. Unlike the other two men, Jasin and Reven had no intentions of going slow. They both liked it fast and hard and a little rough, and my nails dug into Jasin's arms as they pounded me together. They rocked me back and forth, giving and taking, sliding in and out in a rhythm that got faster and faster. They were fire and ice, cool and hot, and I burned and melted all at once between them.

Jasin claimed my mouth while Reven buried his face against my shoulder, and all I could do was cling to them as I came so hard I was sure my cries could be heard by everyone in the nearby tents. The two men let go at the same time, losing control for that brief instant, giving everything to me.

At first, all we could do was hold onto each other and try to breathe, sweat dripping down our bodies, which were still joined together. Slade and Auric grinned at us from the makeshift bed on the floor and patted it in an invitation to join them.

Jasin and Reven carefully lowered me down into the arms of the other men, who helped me get comfortable in my slightly dazed state. All four of them wrapped themselves around me, a combination of coolness and warmth, and I kissed each of them slowly.

"I love you all," I said, as the bond flared bright, so strong I could almost see it filling the room. Each one of my mates told me they loved me too, and I knew that whatever happened tomorrow, they were with me until the end.

32

JASIN

The sun breaching the horizon made the clouds above us look as red as blood. An ominous sign, if one believed in such things. I didn't, of course, but it certainly set the mood as I gazed across the sea of troops lined up in front of me. Soon the field before the Spirit Temple would be covered in their blood, all so we would have a chance to defeat the Dragons.

The plan relied on the soldiers buying us time so we could get inside the Spirit Temple and defeat the Black Dragon as quickly as possible. None of us had any idea what would happen after that, especially once the Spirit Goddess was freed. The Water God had made it sound like the Gods would help us split the Goddess's essences, but nothing was certain.

The Spirit Temple rose before us at the end of the plain

on a hill, nestled up against the mountains beside a waterfall that fed into a clear lake. The temple shimmered where sunlight touched it, due to the walls made from a pale marble that looked like pearl or shell...or maybe bone. Great columns held it up on every corner with ivy and roses twining around them. Above the grand entrance a relief depicted animals, plants, elementals, and dragons, though it was hard to make out the details from a distance. A beautiful garden surrounded the temple, filled with fruit trees, vegetables, and flowers, while the waterfall splashed beside it into a stream that fed down into the valley.

The plains in front of the temple were flat and rich with good soil and thick vegetation. I'd been told that they'd been covered with herds of wild animals until the soldiers arrived. Now the animals had scattered, and the two armies faced each other across their former home.

The Black Dragon's army stretched far and wide, blocking entrance to the Spirit Temple. Onyx Army soldiers in their gleaming black armor waited for the command to attack, lined up in columns that were all too familiar to me. Red, blue, and green markings flashed on their shoulders, along with a few sporting yellow. If the Fire God had chosen another as his Dragon, I'd probably be with them now, wishing I were anywhere else.

On either side of them, dark shadowy figures hovered off the ground, their eerily glowing eyes staring across the field. There were hundreds of shades, more than I'd ever seen before, and the sight of them sent a chill down my spine.

Their deadly hunger was palpable even from a distance, and they wanted nothing more than to drain the life from every person who stood behind me.

Today I wore the Onyx Army armor again, except instead of the red markings for the Fire Realm, mine were bright silver—the color we were using to represent Kira. Across the field, dozens of black banners were raised with a silvery dragon in the center and red, blue, green, and yellow corners. The banner of the Silver Dragon and her mates.

Our army was made up of many different people from all over the four Realms. Men and women with armor and weapons stood side by side with people in regular clothes holding torches, buckets of water, or piles of rocks. Everyone had a task, a way they could help to fight the soldiers or the shades, but there was no question that we were outnumbered and outmatched. If the elementals were fighting beside us, we'd stand a better chance—but they were not. We'd have to do the best we could with what we had.

Garet signaled that they were ready, and I moved to stand in the middle of the field, facing our army. Once there, I shifted into my dragon form, while Kira's other mates stretched out beside me and did the same. Kira walked over wearing her fighting gear with a flowing silver cloak, her glowing sword on her hip. When my red scales flashed under the sunlight she climbed onto my back. I spread my wings and took to the sky, hovering over our soldiers.

"The Black Dragon and her men have ruled over this world for too long," I called out, my dragon voice louder than mine could ever be. "They were meant to protect us, and instead they oppressed us. They were meant to bring peace and order, and instead they brought death and chaos. They were meant to serve the Gods, and instead they imprisoned them. It's time for new Dragons to rise."

Auric, Reven, and Slade flew into the air beside me at those words and let out ear-splitting roars that echoed across the land. The soldiers below us raised their weapons and shouted and cheered, their energy growing with their fervor. Kira had asked me to give this speech, to become the leader the Fire God had told me to be, and though I'd been reluctant at first, I was ready to embrace my destiny as Kira's General. Kira was their symbol, the thing they fought behind, but I would be the one leading them into battle.

"Today we fight for the Silver Dragon," I roared. "We fight for freedom, justice, and equality. We fight for the four Realms. We fight for the Gods. And most of all, we fight for the future of our people." I spread my wings wide. "Today the Black Dragon will be defeated, and the Silver Dragon will ascend!"

The cheers and shouts grew louder, and the army started forward across the field into the fog Auric and Reven had summoned, hiding their numbers. Ahead of them, pools of lava waited for the other army, courtesy of me and Slade. Below us, I spotted Calla and her priests, ready to fight the shades. Garet led the soldiers, directing them to march ahead. The Resistance, the bandits, and the assassins filled in the gaps, while Faya stood in the back with Brin and Leni at her side, all of them looking fierce. As I gazed down at them, I truly believed we could win this battle.

Until the Black Dragon emerged from the Spirit Temple.

33

KIRA

A massive dragon with scales the color of midnight filled the sky, blocking out the sun. Storm clouds surrounded her, lightning flashed behind her, hail fell around her, and the ground beneath her rumbled. The sky turned dark and ominous, and the other four Dragons flew to her side. My heart clenched at the sight of my father with them.

I'd never seen the Black Dragon as anything other than human before, and she was truly terrifying like this. Her claws and talons were razor sharp, and dark, deadly power emanated from her, much like it did from the shades. I found myself gripping Jasin's scales tighter as fear spread through me.

When she spoke, her voice echoed across the plains. "Surrender now and your deaths will be quick and painless.

Fight, and my shades will feast on your souls while my Dragons rip you to shreds."

Her words were probably supposed to make me want to run away, and though I was terrified, all they did was make me angry—and even more determined. I raised my sword into the air and reached for the power inside me. A bright silver light appeared and stretched high into the sky, casting a glow over my assembled army and breaking through the darkness. "We will never surrender! Your time is at an end!"

Her green eyes narrowed. "Then you shall meet your doom."

As soon as she spoke the words she dipped down, plummeting toward the ground so fast it only took her seconds to reach it. She stretched her talons wide and scooped up a handful of our soldiers in each fist, then reared back into the sky. I thought she would let the men fall to their deaths, but as they screamed and struggled, she opened her mouth and a stream of darkness began to flow from their mouths into hers. One by one the soldiers' heads drooped, their bodies becoming lifeless, while my mother's scales seemed to become blacker and blacker.

"She's draining them," I whispered, horrified at what I was seeing.

"And taking their life to fuel her own power," Jasin said, as Nysa opened her claws and let the bodies drop to the ground, one by one.

How were we supposed to stop her? She had no weaknesses. She could control all the elements, and thus was immune to them. She could drain the life of anyone she touched and it only made her stronger. We had no way to defeat her. And even if we did, we'd have to face the Spirit Goddess next.

Her soldiers and shades lurched forward, clashing with our army. The sounds of battle began to ring out, while the storm raged on around us, casting lightning and hail at our soldiers. I spread my arms and reached for it with my magic, calming the raging elements until the clouds began to dissipate, and the sun shined through again.

But the storm was only the beginning of our problems. While the soldiers and shades fought, Sark spewed flame, Heldor ripped open huge trenches in the ground, and Isen created a tornado to tear through our ranks. My own mates dashed forward to combat them, finding the other Dragon they were strongest—and weakest—against, the way Doran had taught them.

Doran...my eyes searched the battle for him, but he wasn't attacking our army. Where did he go?

As Nysa swooped down again to reach for more lives to drain, another dragon slammed into her, knocking her back. They hit the ground in a tangle of black and blue scales, claws and fangs flashing.

My heart leapt into my throat. "Father!" I screamed.

He was actually fighting her, even with the bond between them. His words came back to me. *You're my daughter. Whatever happens, I'm on your side. Always.*

He hadn't betrayed us. He'd been doing everything he could to get close to Nysa again, to win back her trust, so that he could surprise her in this moment. Nysa did have one weakness—her own mates. She wouldn't kill one of her own, not without making herself vulnerable. Doran couldn't kill her either, not without killing himself in the process, but he could distract her for a while to give us a chance.

"Doran is buying us time!" I called out to Jasin. "We have to take out the other Dragons."

"We should get to the Spirit Temple," he said. "The Dragons will follow us and that will give our soldiers a better chance."

"Let's go. Hurry!"

He took off, darting toward the Spirit Temple. Lightning streaked toward us, but I directed it away before it could hit Jasin's wings. He spun and dove, avoiding the numerous elemental attacks flying through the air, and I held on tight. In the chaos I lost track of my other mates, though I knew they were out there, fighting the other Dragons.

Below us, Calla threw fire at the shades around her, while her priests and other people fought with torches, water, and rocks—but it wasn't enough. The dark, ghostly figures swarmed over them, draining their lives, and I knew it wouldn't be long before Calla and her priests succumbed too. And once they were gone, there was little to stop the shades from devouring the rest of our people.

"Wait," I called out to Jasin. "We have to help them fight the shades or they'll never make it."

"We don't have time!"

"We can't let them all die!"

Jasin let out a frustrated roar, but then he changed direction, darting down. As we flew over the shades, he let out a stream of fire while I blasted them with lightning and ice. They let out horrifying shrieks as they disappeared, but more filled their place almost instantly.

We fought and we fought, but as I took in the battle around us, my hope of victory quickly diminished. We were stretched too thin and the other Dragons were too strong. There were too many shades, too many soldiers, and not enough people on our side to fight them back. Getting to the Spirit Temple would be impossible without sacrificing the lives of everyone fighting for us on the battlefield. Was that what it would take?

I couldn't do it. Which meant we were going to fail.

I prepared myself to make a tough decision, though I wasn't sure if it would be to retreat or to push forward. But then a bright flare shot up from the crest of the southern mountain, drawing my attention. A fire burned, spreading wider and wider across the rocky slopes.

No, not a fire, I realized, my breath catching in my throat. Fire elementals.

They were moving fast, gliding over the land as they approached, and there were hundreds of them. Not just fire, but earth, air, and water elementals, all heading toward us at speeds that only a dragon could match.

"They came." Tears filled my eyes and I let out a soft laugh, the relief making me almost giddy. Somehow I had gotten through to them, and they'd changed their minds and decided to fight. And with their help, we might actually stand a chance.

34

KIRA

A surge of hope renewed my energy and Jasin and I fought back the shades until the elementals joined the fray. Our new allies struck down the shades with ease, along with many of the Black Dragon's soldiers who weren't prepared to battle such things. Our soldiers shied away at first, hesitant about the elementals, but then rallied when they realized they were on our side.

Once I was sure the elementals had it under control, I touched Jasin's neck to get his attention. "To the Spirit Temple!"

He let out a roar in response and spread his wings, lifting us over the battlefield to fly toward the shimmering building ahead of us. The other Dragons were still fighting, and elemental attacks flashed through the air, but we rushed past all of them. As we approached the temple, I saw the entrance was sealed with stone, and there seemed no other way inside. With my earth magic I blasted the barrier apart, sending rocks flying, and Jasin dove for the hole I'd made.

Another dragon let out a shriek and a tornado suddenly slammed into Jasin, knocking me off his back. I flew through the air in a daze, trying to breathe, scrambling to grab hold of something. Then my training kicked in and I gathered the air around me, stopping my fall and lifting me higher into the sky.

As I hovered there, a dark green dragon flew toward me. I leaped onto Slade's back, and he sped toward the temple. With his great size he was slower than Jasin, but we managed to fly through the entrance and come to a halt inside.

Jasin and Isen were right at our heels, both of them crashing into the floor with heavy thuds that sent cracks through the marble. Isen was up first, his lithe golden body twisting to attack Jasin with his claws, but Slade blocked him with his own larger frame. My Emerald Dragon let out a deep roar that made the entire temple tremble, and the marble below us split open down a line from him to Isen. The other dragon leaped into the air to avoid the attack, before throwing a lightning bolt at Slade.

Slade shifted back into a human, decreasing his size instantly, and rolled out of the way—a trick we'd learned from Doran. He yanked his axe off his back and charged forward with a shout, his eyes wild. Isen knocked Slade back with his tail, but then Jasin tackled him, tearing into his side with his claws. I trapped Isen's front and back legs with earth magic, forming stone around them so that he was unable to move. He struggled against me and I added ice, making it creep up his body, but he was so strong I knew I couldn't hold him for long.

"Now, Slade!" I yelled.

Slade's axe flashed with a glow the color of fresh leaves before he swung it at Isen's chest. The Golden Dragon let out a piercing shriek as the blade cut through his scales, fueled by Slade's own magic. Isen thrashed and fought with everything he had, blasting us with lightning and wind that sent us flying back, but we didn't stop.

Where the axe touched Isen, stone began to form. Dark gray slate quickly spread across his body, covering the golden scales, while his ear-piercing howls continued. When the stone covered his face, the Golden Dragon finally went silent.

Slade yanked his axe from Isen's chest. As soon as it was removed the dragon's body broke apart, crumbling into hundreds of pieces of rubble at our feet.

A soul-rending scream filled our ears from outside the Spirit Temple, so loud and horrifying it could only be from the Black Dragon herself. She'd sensed her mate had died, and although I empathized with how much pain and suffering she must be going through, I didn't feel bad for what we'd done.

As if responding to her screams, the temple walls on every side of us suddenly burst apart in a spray of stone and dust. It covered us, blinded us, and filled our lungs. When I could see again, I realized she'd torn open the temple's walls, leaving only the roof and the columns holding it up. What had once been a beautiful building was now little more than ruins, which looked as though they might collapse at any moment. Gods, the Black Dragon was powerful. Too powerful, even now with one of her mates gone.

Now that the temple was open to the world on every side, I could see the other Dragons fighting under the hazy sky. Sark and Reven shot fire and ice at each other, both moving so quickly they were little more than a blur. The Black Dragon tossed my father aside, causing him to hit the rocky mountain behind the temple, where he fell and crashed into the stream below. She then soared back into the thick of the battle, grabbing more of our soldiers in her talons to drain their lives. We had to stop her quickly.

A huge green dragon slammed against the floor of the temple in front of me, his wings spread so wide it blocked out everything else. "You'll pay for what you've done," Heldor growled.

He snapped at me with his fangs, but then Auric was there, yanking me out of the way with his air magic. He blocked me with his golden body and faced Heldor down, while Jasin and Slade moved in from either side. Four huge dragons ready to fight, and me standing in the middle of them.

"Go," Auric told me. "Help Reven. We've got this one."

I sheathed my sword and ran out of the temple, or what was left of it anyway. As the plains below me came into a view, I stared at the destruction before me, the revulsion from so much death nearly overpowering my senses. It was against everything my life magic stood for, and it took all my power not to run away. The Black Dragon fed on death and misery, eating the darkness and becoming stronger. It was time to take away more of her powers and end this nightmare forever.

35

REVEN

I felt a tug through the bond, urging me to go to Kira, and I changed course immediately to swoop down toward her. She stood in front of the crumbling temple, covered in pale dust, making her red hair appear almost white. As I drew near, she leaped onto my back, her eyes blazing with determination.

"Let's stop Sark, once and for all," she said.

A grin spread across my face, making my fangs emerge. Sark had taken everything from us—and now he was going to pay. "I was thinking the exact same thing."

I launched us into the air, the wind whipping at my wings. Sark rose before us, his blood red body shining under the sun. Hatred filled my chest, along with my need for vengeance, but I didn't let it consume me. This wasn't only about revenge or justice. This was about stopping him from hurting anyone else.

My body was already burnt in three places, and my ice had torn through the scales on Sark's back. We'd already been fighting for what felt like hours, but neither of us could best the other. With Kira by my side, that might change.

The Crimson Dragon opened his mouth and scorching hot fire flew toward us. I let out a stream of water from my own mouth to combat it, while Kira threw bolts of lightning and blades of ice at Sark. He managed to dodge them all, moving unnaturally fast despite his size. In both forms he was an expert of combat, and he'd had many years to hone his skills. He was the one fighter I was willing to admit might be even better than me.

Across the field, the Black Dragon suddenly let out another of her terrible screams, which tore through my ears, struck me in the heart, and ripped through my bones. Balls of fire suddenly rained down from the sky, as if the sun itself was attacking us, and soldiers below us screamed in agony as they hit the fields and consumed them. Kira did her best to stop more flames from falling or the fires from spreading, while I blasted what I could with water, but it was too much for us to handle. The Black Dragon's magic was too strong, fueled by her pain over her mates' deaths and the lives she'd been stealing.

She fixed her beady black eyes on the temple and suddenly rushed toward it, flying so fast she was little more than a dark blur. A spike of panic shot through me. Auric, Jasin, and Slade were in there, and they were no match for her. Doran flew after Nysa only seconds later, but one of his wings appeared to be injured, slowing him down. They might be able to distract her for a short time, but that was all.

"Heldor must have fallen," Kira said.

"We need to take out Sark now!" I called to her.

"Get me close to him!"

Sark was momentarily stunned by the death of Heldor, but he quickly recovered and let out a roar of his own. He blasted us with unending fire, but I wove through his attacks, while Kira deflected them away from us. But every time I tried to get close to him, he darted away.

I reached for Auric's magic through the bond and summoned thick clouds around us, hiding us from Sark's gaze. He tried to burn them up with streams of fire, searching for us in the haze, and I flew past him, then swept back around. I approached him from behind as quietly as possible and drew up alongside him.

Kira launched herself off my back, using her air magic to guide her onto Sark's crimson body. As she landed, he spun around and let out a harsh shriek, while she held on tight so she wouldn't fall. He swiped for her with his claws, but she drew her sword and stabbed it into his back, forcing him to release another pained roar. Ice began to form around the wound, but then his entire body erupted into flames and melted the ice.

The bastard wouldn't die, and I worried he would hurt Kira if this continued. She was immune to his fire, but not his fangs or claws. She yanked at her sword, unable to budge it from his scales, as he tried to knock her off him and slashed at her.

I flew up high then dove down toward him, pressing my wings close to my side. When I was seconds away from slamming into him, I shifted into human form, my black cloak flying behind me as I drew my swords. Flames scorched me and I covered myself with a layer of ice, but it quickly melted away. I had no air magic to guide me, but I landed on his back beside Kira, and stabbed both my swords into his thick neck.

Sark let out an unholy scream and the flames shot higher, burning me despite my own magic's protection, but I refused to let go.

"This is for my family," I said, as I dug my father's twin blades deeper into Sark's neck. Ice spread from the dual blades and across his body, consuming the flames. As his body froze, he tried to knock us off him, his wings beating at the sky and his talons reaching for us, fighting until the very end.

The last bit of life left Sark as the tips of his wings froze, and we began to plummet to the ground. Another mournful, horrible scream came from the Spirit Temple as the world rushed up at us. We were too low for me to safely turn to a dragon—we'd hit the ground before I could raise my wings.

Kira grabbed me around the waist, and I felt her magic wrap around us. We jumped off Sark's back just before he struck the earth with a heavy thud. His body cracked into a million pieces of ice at the impact, and they all exploded outward with dirt and grass from the garden where he'd crashed. Kira and I leaped wide, her air magic guiding our landing, taking us away from the danger and safely planting us on a patch of grass nearby.

I straightened up and brushed myself off, while eyeing Kira to make sure she was all right. My clothes and magic had melted into my skin from the knee down, and now that the fight was over the pain from my burned and blackened skin became agony. None of that mattered though, because Sark was gone. The millions of pieces of ice that had once been his body melted away under the dim sunlight and sank into the earth, and the weight of my families' deaths lifted off me. They were avenged, along with Kira's family and friends, and everyone else who had lost their loved ones to the Black Dragon's enforcer.

"Three Dragons defeated," Kira said, with something like awe or disbelief in her voice as she stared at the Spirit Temple's remains.

"The Black Dragon must be weakened now," I said.

She took my hand and clenched it tight. "Time to face her."

36

KIRA

The second I touched Reven I realized how badly he'd been hurt by Sark's fires. He stumbled forward anyway, but his feet and legs were so burned it must have been excruciating. Still, he shifted into his dragon form, his scales blackened in many places, and lowered himself so I could climb onto his back.

"You're hurt," I said, as I got on.

"We'll worry about that later," he said through gritted teeth.

As he took off, I placed my hands on his scales, knowing I wouldn't be able to do enough to heal him, but hoping it would ease the pain. He flew into the open space between the columns of the Spirit Temple, where dragons fought, and magic flew.

Doran, Auric, and Slade all surrounded Nysa, who bared her fangs and hissed at them, before lashing out with ice and a swipe of her claws. If she touched them, she'd be able to use her death magic against them and drain their lives. Jasin was crumpled against a pillar, unconscious, injured, and in his human form.

Every time one of my mates got a blow in with their air or earth magic, I felt a sense of hope—before watching Nysa's scales heal themselves almost immediately. She wasn't immune to fire, earth, or air anymore, but the Spirit Goddess inside her made her powerful anyway. And with Doran's water magic too, she was nearly unstoppable.

"Protect Jasin!" I told Reven, as I hopped off his back. I knew he would never listen if I told him to stand back and rest, but he might do this for me. "She still has water magic, and Jasin is weak against it!"

Reven hesitated, clearly itching to fight, but then let out a snarl and stomped over to stand guard over Jasin's unconscious body. As he did, Slade was thrown back against one of the huge columns, bolts of ice piercing his wings. He hit the ground with a heavy thud that shook the foundation of the temple, sending debris falling from the cracked and broken ceiling.

I rushed into the battle just as Auric was tackled by my mother, her talons tearing into his scaled back, making him cry out. Ice formed around his body, holding him in place, and she opened her mouth to drain his life. I drew my sword and rushed her with a yell, desperate to save my mate, but she slapped me with her tail and sent me flying, along with my sword.

As I hit the ground, Doran slammed into Nysa's body,

knocking her into a pillar. It snapped under her weight and part of the roof caved in on her. But I knew she'd be back up soon.

All of my dragons were injured. I felt their pain through the bond, and there was nothing I could do about it. The Black Dragon was too strong for us to defeat—but I had to try anyway.

Doran flowed into his human form and bent down to pick up my sword. His hazel eyes met mine as he gripped it tight. "There's only one of her mates left now."

I realized at that instant what he was about to do and panic gripped my throat. "Don't do this! There has to be another way!"

"We both know there isn't. I love you, Kira."

"Father, no!" I yelled as he stabbed the sword into his chest. Fire spread across his body instantly, engulfing him completely. I rushed toward him and made it to my father's side seconds after he hit the ground, but by then it was already too late.

Through the fire I cradled Doran's head in my hands, tears leaking down my face, as the light left his eyes. I'd once hated and feared him, and then I'd doubted him, and then I'd grown to love him. He knew I would never be able to kill him, even after he seemingly betrayed us, and he'd given his own life so we would have a chance.

As the fire vanished, I buried my head in my father's chest, letting myself sob, my hands covered in his blood. Nysa screamed behind me, her voice filled with pain as she reared up out of the debris. I could only imagine how bad it must hurt to feel every single one of your mates' deaths. I wished with every breath that it hadn't come to this—or that I didn't have to defeat my own mother now.

Enva's words came back to me and I wondered if it was true that Nysa, deep down, didn't want to fight me and just wanted this all to end. She hadn't attacked me so far, and she hadn't killed my mates. Maybe it was true. Maybe I could find a way to break through to her and convince her to stop.

I pressed a kiss to my father's burnt forehead and whispered, "I love you too." Then I pulled my sword from his chest and turned to face my mother.

Nysa stomped out of the rubble and shook it off, her tail whipping about her and her wings raised. Shadows clung to her black scales and her eyes glowed like the shades outside. She looked like she was about to tear the entire world down.

I moved in front of her, my sword at my side, and yelled, "Mother!"

She gazed down at me like I was an insignificant bug in her path, one that she could stomp at any moment. "You," she said, putting so much venom in the word it burned me.

"I don't want to fight you, mother, and I don't think you want to fight me either. Neither one of us has to die today."

"You're wrong," she said, yet she didn't move to attack me.

Hope surged inside me and I stepped forward. "Free the Spirit Goddess and we can work together to defeat her. With the Gods' help, we can split her into Life and Death, and send Death back to the Realm of the Dead."

She dipped her head low, her sharp fangs glistening as they drew near. "You killed my mates," she hissed. "And now I shall do the same to yours."

She brought one of her huge clawed feet down on me, pinning me to the ground with her talons. As she loomed over me, she opened her mouth wide and began to drain my life—along with my mates' through our bond. Inky blackness squirmed up from my throat and into her, making me weak. With my life being sucked out of me I couldn't move, couldn't breathe, couldn't fight—I was going to die at the hands of my own mother.

Suddenly a wave as tall as the temple crashed into her, knocking her off me. Reven stumbled toward her in his dragon form, assaulting her with non-stop water, giving me a chance to recover. I drew in a deep breath as I got to my feet and reached for my life magic, letting it restore me.

There was no reasoning with Nysa. Whatever goodness that had once been inside of her was gone, lost to the corruption that had taken hold of her. It was time to save her from what she'd become.

I summoned all of the elements at once, causing my body to rise up into the air while fire and water swirled around me and huge chunks of the temple's marble lifted to my side. Lightning danced in my hair. Lava gathered at my fingertips. Fog spread through the temple.

My mates moved behind me, facing Nysa down, each one battered and broken but still fighting. They gathered their magic and reached through the bond that linked us all to fortify it.

My connection with my mates gave me strength. The blessings of the Gods gave me power. Love and compassion gave me purpose. I collected all of that inside me, and then I released it at her, hitting her with every element. My mates joined in, blasting her from every side, making her arch her wings and scream. Fire and ice, earth and wind, lightning and lava, steam and storm—it all converged on her in one final push.

I reached out with my air magic and grabbed hold of my sword while Nysa's body tried to heal the damage we inflicted on her. All four elements inside my blade leaped to my command and the sword flew through the air, hitting Nysa in the heart. It buried deep into her chest, and every element spread out from it, washing over her one by one.

She reared up and I prepared to strike again, worried it wouldn't be enough—but then her body changed. She resumed her human form, so small and unassuming compared to the dragon she'd once been, and then collapsed.

My magic vanished and I hit the floor, then took off running toward her. The hilt of my sword protruded from her chest, but she still managed to cling to life, even as black blood seeped onto the cracked marble. I kneeled over her, and her eyes met mine.

"You don't know what you've done." Her voice was a gravely whisper laced with pain.

"I'm sorry," I said, my throat closing with emotion. "I wish it didn't have to end like this."

"When I die, she'll be released." My mother coughed up blood, turned to the side, and spat it on the floor. "I'm the only thing holding her back, even now. When I let go, there will be no stopping her."

I couldn't help but rest my hand upon her head, touching the hair that looked so much like my own. "Rest now. You've held her long enough. The Gods will help us."

"The Gods." She let out a bitter laugh. "The Gods lie."

I didn't know what to say to that, so I simply stroked her head as the life drained out of her. I sensed my mates moving behind me, but they gave us space.

"Forgive me, Kira," my mother said, her voice weakening. "It was the only way."

Her eyes fluttered shut, and with one last gasp, she was gone.

37

KIRA

The black blood pooling on the ground beneath Nysa began to move. At first it was only a few drops darting across the floor, small enough to make me think it was a trick of the light. But then more blood joined it in a flowing line, before converging in the center of the temple. I backed away from Nysa's body slowly as it was drained, and the puddle before me grew and grew. It lifted up and began to take form, becoming a massive dragon that filled the temple with inky darkness.

"Get ready," I told my mates, who were all in their human forms now.

They spread out around the Spirit Goddess as her body dripped black blood. She raised her head and let out a terrifying roar that shook the world.

One by one the Gods appeared. The volcanic Fire God,

made of lava and ash. The stormy Air God. The sparkling, crystalized Earth God. And finally, the fluid Water God.

The Spirit Goddess swung her head around, taking in the temple and her Gods. "After centuries of imprisonment I am finally free."

Power seeped from her body with every bit of dark blood that dripped down her limbs. Revulsion, dread, and a sense of wrongness made me bend over and gag. It was like touching the bone cage, but a thousand times worse. My instincts screamed at me that this was unnatural, that I needed to get away from it as quickly as possible, but I couldn't run from this. I had to face her.

"You must split the two halves of the Spirit Goddess," I told the Gods, trying not to gag again. "Hurry!"

"No," the Fire God said, with a finality in his voice that made me tremble.

"No?" Reven asked.

"We have no wish for her to be separated again," the Fire God said. "Like this, she is whole."

"She's been corrupted," Auric said. "There's barely any life left in her, only death."

"She is our mate," the Earth God said, his voice a deep rumble.

"But you said you would help us separate the Life and Death sides of her," Jasin said.

"We needed you to defeat the Dragons so that our Goddess would be freed," the Water God said.

"You lied to us," Slade said.

"We are the Gods, and you are meant to serve us," the Air God said. "This is why we chose you."

The Spirit Goddess loomed over us, making me feel small and insignificant. "It's time for the Gods to return to power. We've been forgotten for too long, but we shall be worshipped again." She snarled at us. "Now kneel."

Nysa was right—the Gods had lied to us. We'd made a mistake by trusting them. They were just as corrupted as the Spirit Goddess was, just as Nysa's mates had been corrupted too. But unlike Nysa and her Dragons, there was no way to kill a God. They'd created us and gave us a small fraction of their powers. We didn't stand a chance against them.

There was only one thing for me to do.

"We will never kneel," I said.

"Then you will die." The Spirit Goddess wrapped one of her claws around me and lifted me into the air. "We no longer need the Dragons."

At the Spirit Goddess's touch, the revulsion became so strong I thought I might pass out, but I pushed through it. "Do it now!" I yelled at my Dragons.

My mates each formed a ring around the Gods using their elements. Doran had given them a quick lesson in how to imprison the Gods, and though it would be more effective in the temples, this would hold them temporarily. As the fire danced around Jasin, he yelled, "Water God, I bind you in fire!" Auric imprisoned the Earth God at the same moment, the wind whipping his hair around, while Slade and Reven did the same to the Air and Fire Gods.

With the Gods imprisoned, the Spirit Goddess was

231

weakened. But instead of fighting her, I drew her into me. It was like the opposite of healing my mates. For them, I gave up some of my life magic and my energy. Now I grabbed hold of the life and death magic that surrounded me and sucked it in. I drained the Spirit Goddess, like the Black Dragon had drained the lives of my soldiers.

Her body broke apart into black blood, which streamed into my mouth, my eyes, my nose, my ears. Her essence blasted me so strong my arms flew to my sides, my body buffeted by the nonstop stream of magic that coursed through me. I hovered in the air as every last drop of that disgusting blood filled me.

In the distance I heard yelling and saw magic flying, but nothing could hurt me now. Anything that dared to injure me I healed instantly. Not even the other Gods could stand against me now.

"Stop, Kira!" Jasin yelled.

"Don't do this!" Slade called out.

"This is the only way," I told them, my voice booming around us. "She must be contained."

They didn't understand. They couldn't feel her like I could. If she was allowed to remain free, she would destroy the world. The second she entered my body I'd known it. And if the Gods wouldn't help us divide her, imprisonment was the only way.

When the last drop of black blood entered me, power unlike anything I'd ever known spread through my consciousness. All I knew was darkness, death, and a hunger that could never be satisfied. But deep inside that thick shroud was a small light, a spark of life, a fluttering of hope. I tried to reach for it, but was quickly overwhelmed by death again.

I gazed across my ruined temple, seeing beyond it, feeling the dead soldiers outside, the ones that were injured, and the ones still fighting and full of life. They were all mine. I was more powerful than any other being in this world. Stronger than the Dragons or the other Gods. I was the beginning and the end, life and death, darkness and light. I controlled shades and elementals, plants and animals, the living and the dead, and soon they would all bow to me. I would use this power to reshape the world. A dark queen, ruling all five Realms with my mates at my side.

I heard people yelling my name over and over, their voices frantic. I focused on them again, the four handsome men I'd taken as my lovers, and recognition slowly dawned. Something of myself fought for control again.

"Kira, you have to let her go!" Jasin yelled.

I shook my head. "I can't. She'll destroy everyone if she's free. She hungers for death and will never be sated until this world is in ruins."

"Don't make the same mistakes your mother made," Auric said.

"I won't. I can contain the Spirit Goddess without becoming corrupted, and then we can use her power to change the world."

"You might be able to fight her for a few years," Slade said. "But she'll corrupt all of us eventually."

"No!" I roared, both at them and at the Spirit Goddess

inside me who fought for control. I couldn't let her win. I wouldn't!

"Kira, you have to fight her!" Reven yelled.

I screamed and covered my head with my hands, the power threatening to tear me apart. Clarity dawned and for an instant I was Kira again. "I can't—she's too strong!"

"Yes, you can," Reven said, staring into my eyes. "Otherwise you'll have to live countless lives with the Spirit Goddess inside you. Killing your own children to keep her contained. Are you willing to do that?"

"No—never!"

"Then fight!"

I reached again for that tiny flicker of life inside me, and this time I found it. I grabbed hold and yanked, dragging it through the darkness, fighting with every ounce of my being against the black death trying to consume me.

Enva's voice suddenly drifted to me, like a whisper on the wind. "Don't give up, Kira."

"Enva!" I cried, begging for her to help me, though I knew she couldn't.

She appeared before me, her form translucent and glowing with a faint silver light. "I'm here."

Other people began to appear alongside her, with the same silvery bodies and pale glowing eyes, like the opposite of the shades outside. Nysa appeared first, looking young, bright, and brave. Doran stood at her side, his eyes proud as he smiled at me. Sark, Heldor, and Isen stood behind them, their features lacking the cruelty I'd seen before. This must have been how they'd looked before they were corrupted.

But then more luminous figures appeared beside me, standing close, forming a tight circle around me. Young women I felt a strong connection to, though I'd never seen them before. *Sisters*, a voice deep in my soul whispered in recognition. Nysa's other daughters, stretching back centuries, freed now that she was dead. They gave me their strength and their unconditional love, and their silent encouragement and support gave me hope.

In front of them stood a woman with long red hair, hazel eyes, and features identical to my own. I faced a mirror image of myself.

Sora, my twin sister.

"Kira," she said. "We're here to help you."

"How?"

"Together we can divide the Spirit Goddess into her two halves. I am death, while you are life." She smiled at me as she took my hands. "From the beginning, it was always meant to be this way."

I swallowed, my fingers tightening around hers. "I'm not strong enough."

"You are. Focus on the life inside you, and I'll draw out the death. We can do this together."

"You're not alone," Enva called out.

"We'll give you our power," Nysa said.

"You can do this, Kira," my father added.

Their magic suddenly filled me, until I was overflowing with life and light and love. They sent me so much power it began to balance out the darkness inside me and let the buried life magic grow. I sensed the two halves of the Spirit

Goddess within me and held tight to the side of life. My twin tightened her grip on my hands and opened her mouth, drawing out the darkness from within me. It flowed out of me and filled her up, but where it had corrupted me, she was able to stay in control of herself. She'd been born with the power of death from the beginning, and now she fed upon it,

The Spirit Goddess fought inside me, trying to stay whole, while her Gods yelled and fought my mates keeping them prisoner. Sora and I managed to hold on, backed by the magic of our sisters and our parents, and I felt lighter and lighter with each second. When the last bit of death's essence had left me, my sister released my hands. The connection was broken. The Spirit Goddess was split in two, each part of her trapped within my sister and me.

"Now it's time to open the gates to the Realm of the Dead and send everyone home," my sister said, her voice thick with dark power. "Including the Death Goddess."

A blast of dark magic erupted from her, and one by one our sisters took on a look of relief before vanishing. Sora had opened the gates to the Realm of the Dead, allowing all the departed souls to finally pass through and find peace.

"I don't want you to go," I said. "I only just found you."

"I am with you always, Kira. Life and death will eternally be joined together. But now I must take the Death Goddess back to where she belongs."

I nodded, a tear slipping down my cheek. Sora gave me a warm smile, and then she disappeared.

Enva wrapped her arms around me next. "I knew you could save us all. Goodbye, granddaughter."

Before I could reply she faded away, her face looking truly peaceful for the first time. Tears streamed down my face, my heart torn between happiness and sadness. I'd never see them again, but their suffering was finally at an end.

Sark, Isen, and Heldor bowed their heads low to me in a sign of respect, before they disappeared, leaving Doran behind.

My father placed a hand on my shoulder. "I'm proud of you, Kira."

I turned to hug him, choking back a sob. "I couldn't have done it without you."

He patted my back once before drifting away. There was only one ghost left.

"You're going to make a fine Dragon," Nysa said, her translucent hand reaching toward me to curl around my cheek. I placed my hand over hers for just an instant, before she left me with the words, "Thank you for freeing me. I love you, Kira."

After she vanished, the temple was empty except for my mates and the Gods they held prisoner. Inside me, all I felt was the Life Goddess, who was relieved to finally be herself again, untainted by corruption. I searched deep inside and found nothing left of the darkness.

I took a deep breath...and I released her.

Light flowed out of me and formed a beautiful, shining dragon, so bright it nearly hurt to look at her. Flowers bloomed at her feet, and she gazed down at me with a motherly smile.

"Is it over?" I asked.

"It's never over," the Life Goddess said, her voice warm and comforting. "Life and death fight an eternal battle, and one cannot exist without the other. My sister and I will always be connected. But if you mean is she safely trapped in the Realm of the Dead? Then yes."

"Thank Gods," I said, with a sigh of relief.

She let out a laugh that wrapped around me like a warm hug. "No, thank you for freeing me. And now I shall purge my mates of their corruption."

She turned to look at the imprisoned gods and then sent a burst of light out from her. It flowed into them, filling them up, and when it was over they each glowed a little brighter.

"What do we do now?" I asked her. The Gods had said before they wanted to rule without us. Did they still want that?

"You shall continue your duty of bringing balance to the world, while we watch over you from afar. There is much to be done, but we have faith that you are up to the task." She lowered her head and pressed a soft kiss to my forehead that filled me with love and hope. "I give you my blessing."

As she pulled away, my body began to change. I grew larger and stronger, while my hands became claws, my skin became scales, and my teeth became fangs. Glowing silver wings sprouted from my back, and a long tail whipped behind me.

The Life Goddess gave me a nod, her eyes kind, before she disappeared in a flash so bright I had to look away. When the light dimmed, the other Gods were gone too.

"Kira..." Slade placed a large, dark hand on my silver scales. "You did it."

Reven smirked. "I knew you could defeat her."

"I couldn't have done it without all of you." My voice sounded deeper and stronger as a dragon.

Auric stroked my snout. "You're magnificent."

"Let's go end this battle," Jasin said.

The others turned into dragons and we flew out of the ruins of the Spirit Temple, over the battlefield. The shades were gone, taken back to the Realm of the Dead with the Death Goddess, and the Black Dragon's soldiers had already surrendered. I stretched out my senses with my enhanced life magic, which I could access now that the Goddess was freed. There were so many dead, far too many, and many more injured. Zara and Garet had both fallen, much to my dismay. I ached at the thought of telling Auric that his brother was gone, and Zara's death meant the Assassin's Guild was leaderless. Leni was badly wounded, one of her arms severed from her shoulder, and I wasn't sure if she would survive. Slade would be devastated if his little sister passed, and I prayed that she would make it.

There were more casualties that tugged on my heart. Enva was gone, along with the sisters I'd barely gotten to glimpse, including Sora. And of course, the Dragons. Doran had sacrificed himself to give us a chance, proving he was truly a father to me. And Nysa... Well, I understood Nysa a lot better now after encountering the Spirit Goddess. The things she had done could never be truly forgiven, but she was my mother, and she'd tried to protect the world as best she could.

Even with all these losses, there was still so much life—and hope. Elementals and humans had fought side by side, fighting back the darkness that had overtaken our land, and I felt confident this was the beginning of a fresh start for our two races. Other friends were still alive—Brin, who had fought valiantly to protect Faya and her unborn child; Calla and her priests, who had kept the shades at bay for so long; and Cadock, who had led the bandits in a noble fight despite his earlier misgivings. Not to mention hundreds of lives I didn't know but could feel before me, their souls bright lights on the bloody fields.

As the sun sank to the horizon, my Dragons and I flew high and drew the attention of everyone still standing. Faces turned up at us, filled with awe and relief.

"The era of the Black Dragon is over," Jasin called out. "All hail the Silver Dragon!"

The soldiers and elementals below us let out a loud cheer that seemed to echo throughout the entire world. This battle was truly over, but now the work of rebuilding the four Realms would begin.

I turned to my mates, my forever family, who had stood by my side through it all. This wouldn't have been possible without them. The love we had for each other was what brought us our victory today. And whatever happened next? We would be together for it, preparing for the day when our own daughter would take my place.

39

JASIN

ONE YEAR LATER

The sounds of combat rang out all around me. Swords clashing together. Fists hitting flesh. Shouts and muttered curses. I couldn't help but smile as I gazed across the courtyard. Dozens of men and women fought in pairs, practicing and sparring while sweating under the hot sun. Once they had been bandits, Resistance fighters, assassins, or Onyx Army soldiers. Now they were mine.

The Silver Guard, I'd called them. The most loyal and dedicated soldiers, sworn to serve the Silver Dragon as her soldiers now that the Onyx Army had disbanded. Each Realm was transitioning to governing itself with its own military, since Kira had no interest in ruling. Our plan was to work as mediators and guardians of the world, and as part of that I would lead this elite fighting force, which suited me well. As for Kira's other mates, Auric was handling diplomacy with the leaders of the four Realms, Reven was working with the elementals while also managing a team of spies and scouts, while Slade was acting as Kira's right hand man and personal guard. In the end, they weren't that different from the roles Nysa's men held, except our goals were a lot different. We didn't want power or domination, we wanted harmony and peace. Gods knew the world needed it right now.

Other sounds caught my attention, drawing my gaze up toward the hammering, pounding, and yelling. Renovations on Soulspire palace had recently begun to transform it from the run-down, dark, imposing fortress it had been under the Black Dragon's rule to the new home of the Silver Dragon. We'd all been surprised when Kira said she wanted to live here after being imprisoned inside it, but she'd argued that the central location between the four Realms and the long history of housing the Dragons made it the perfect place for us to reside. It just needed some work to make it home.

Cadock walked past the sparring soldiers and made his way toward me. His knee had been injured during the battle at the Spirit Temple and he'd walked with a slight limp ever since, although it hadn't slowed him down much. He wore the bright armor of the Silver Guard and acted as my second in command.

"Training is coming along nicely," I said to him.

"Yes, I think the new recruits will be ready soon."

"How are things with Faya?" I asked. Cadock had become smitten with the former Resistance leader, but after she'd lost her husband to the Dragons she'd been hesitant to start a relationship again, especially while taking care of a baby boy.

He rubbed the back of his neck. "One step forward, two steps back. I love her, and little Parin too. I asked her to marry me and she said maybe someday."

I clasped his shoulder. "You're a good man. She sees that. She just needs time."

"I know. I told her I'd wait as long as it takes. I'm not going anywhere." He drew in a breath. "That's not why I'm here though. There are some people asking to see you."

"Who?"

"They say they're your parents."

My spine stiffened. I hadn't seen or heard from my parents since my father had betrayed me by turning us in to the Onyx Army for helping the Resistance. I'd tried to block them from my memory ever since, too hurt by the knowledge that he was more loyal to the Black Dragon than his own son. What were they doing here now?

I considered sending them away, but I did miss my mother, and I had nothing to fear from my father anymore. The least I could do was see why they had traveled all the way from their home in the Fire Realm to visit me.

"Send them to my office," I said.

Cadock nodded and walked away, while I watched my recruits a little longer, letting their rhythmic fighting movements calm me. I'd never wanted to be a soldier in the Onyx Army, but my parents had made it clear that was my one path, and I'd been damn good at it even though I'd hated it. When I'd met Kira, I'd been ashamed of my past and the things I'd been forced to do, but at her side I was finally able to accept my destiny. I was a protector, and when I fought for something I believed in, I was proud of this work.

I reluctantly turned away from my soldiers and headed for the nearby barracks, where I'd claimed a large room for my office. I'd chosen it because it had windows that looked out at the training grounds and the palace, allowing me to keep an eye on everything. I also liked the lighting in the room—it was good for painting.

My parents were already waiting inside when I arrived. They sat in the two chairs across from my desk but jumped to their feet when I shut the door behind me.

"Mom, Dad," I said. "What are you doing here?"

"Oh, Jasin," my mother said, clasping her hands to her chest. "It's so good to see you."

"Your mother has been worried about you," my father said.

I took her hands in mine and gave them a squeeze. My mother was the only reason I'd escaped when my father had betrayed me, and I'd missed her also. "Please sit down."

I walked around the table as they sat down again. I noticed their eyes drifting to the painting behind me, which depicted the Silver Dragon flying in front of the ruined Spirit Temple, with her other Dragons flanking her. A memory of the day we'd won.

"That's beautiful," Mom said, as I sat across from her. "Did you paint it?"

"I did." Although we'd had a lot to do after the battle at the Spirit Temple, Kira had insisted we take some time for ourselves too. Once the world had settled down a bit, we'd spent two weeks in the middle of nowhere, relaxing and recovering from our ordeals. I'd done that painting then, along with many others, including some I definitely wouldn't want my parents to see.

"It's beautiful," my mother said. "I'm so happy you're painting again."

"Why are you here?" I asked again, pinning my father with a steely gaze.

He shifted in his seat uncomfortably. He looked a lot older than I remembered. "I've come to tell you I deeply regret what I did that day, and I'm sorry. I thought I was helping you."

My eyes narrowed at him. "You turned me in to the Onyx Army. You effectively sealed my death sentence. How is that helping me?"

"General Voor promised you wouldn't be killed, only brought back into the Onyx Army and punished. I hoped you would realize the error of your ways." He shook his head, staring down at his hands. "I see now that I was wrong. About a lot of things. I only hope that one day you'll be able to forgive me."

"We're moving to Soulspire," Mom said, surprising me. "The Fire Realm has nothing left for us except bad memories. We'd like a fresh start somewhere near you."

I crossed my arms, leaning back in my chair. "You think that by moving closer and saying you're sorry I'll forgive your betrayal?"

"No," Dad said. "I only hope that you'll give me a

chance to try to mend things between us. I love you, son, and I'm proud of you. Really damn proud."

I sighed and pinched the bridge of my nose. I disliked my father, but I loved him too, and I missed my mother. In the past, I would have gone into an angry rage and told them to get out of my office, but I'd changed since meeting Kira and the others. Maybe my father could change too.

"I'm not sure forgiveness is possible, but it would be good to see you more often," I said.

My mother's smile made it worthwhile, while my father nodded eagerly. Our relationship might never be what it was, but this was a start in the right direction at least.

After they left, I felt Kira's presence draw near. I stood and walked to the door to greet her with a kiss. She had a blank canvas under her arm.

"Everything all right?" she asked.

"It is now," I said. "What did you bring me?"

She held out the canvas. "I thought a few hours of painting might do you good. You seemed stressed, and that guest room in the west wing of the palace needs an artist's touch."

I chuckled softly as I set the canvas aside and drew her close. "That's very thoughtful of you. But I think I need some inspiration from my muse first."

I pulled her into the room and shut the door with a wry grin. As my lips found her neck and my hands slid down her body, she let out a husky laugh filled with desire. I would never grow tired of that sound—or of loving Kira.

40

AURIC

FIVE YEARS LATER

The gardens outside Soulspire palace were full of people in their finest clothes, all of them chatting with excitement and anticipation as they waited for the wedding to begin. When the music ended a hush went through the crowd and the two brides stepped forward, wearing matching gowns in different colors. Brin's gown was pale yellow and decorated with citrines to represent the Air Realm, while Leni's was the color of fresh new leaves with emeralds for the Earth Realm. The gown was cut so that it didn't hide Leni's missing arm but celebrated it, a reminder of our triumph at the Spirit Temple and everything we'd sacrificed for peace.

With their hands clasped, Brin and Leni moved to stand in front of the altar, which was decorated with crystals, incense, candles, and bowls of water, representing the four elements. Calla, the High Priestess of the Fire God, greeted them both with a smile and began the ceremony.

I watched my best friend as she spoke the words binding her life to Leni's, and I couldn't help but smile. Brin had become one of my advisers in the last few years, helping me with diplomatic relations between the four Realms. After Kira released all the Realms to rule themselves independently, the Air and Water Realms had adapted easily and were eager for this change, but the Earth and Fire Realms had a harder time with it. They'd relied so much on the Black Dragon's control and guidance that they'd struggled without it, but things were getting better now. Brin had been a big part of that.

Leni, on the other hand, worked for Reven. She'd proved to be a good scout and spy, plus she wasn't afraid of the elementals...or anything else, really. And she never let her injury hold her back.

As the ceremony wrapped up, Kira took my hand with a bright smile. I caught Slade's eye and he gave me a warm nod. His large family stood around him, his mother crying happy tears into a handkerchief and his other sister beaming with happiness. Brin's parents were there too looking much more stoic, although they were smiling, and their eyes were bright. They'd accepted their daughter and the woman she loved, even if they'd once wanted me to marry her instead.

When the two women kissed and were proclaimed a married couple, the entire audience cheered. Kira raised a hand and petals of all different colors rained down on the garden like snow, and everyone turned their heads up toward the blessing.

"We never had a wedding," I said to her. "Does that bother you?"

"Not at all," Kira said. "We don't need one. Our souls are bound together for all eternity. That's stronger than any wedding ceremony." She nudged me with her hip. "Besides, we get enough attention as it is. It's nice to have a day honoring our friends instead."

"Yes, it is." I glanced around the garden, which Kira had put in last year to honor the Life Goddess. Hundreds of people now celebrated on its lawn, dancing to the music and congratulating the happy couple. There were elementals among us too, the ambassadors who had been staying in the palace the past few years while the negotiations with their people progressed. Reven had been a big part of that, and though relations with the elementals weren't perfect, they were getting better. He spoke with one of them now while sipping a glass of wine, with Jasin beside him nodding at something he said.

Behind them, I caught sight of Cadock and Faya dancing with her son Parin, now about five years old. They'd gotten married two years ago, and Faya was pregnant with her second child now. She was another of my advisers, helping me with the Earth Realm in particular. As Cadock picked up Parin I noticed his slight limp, another reminder of our victory and everything we'd lost to achieve it. A touch of old sadness struck me as I remembered my brother Garet, who'd also fallen that day. I knew he would be proud of what we'd accomplished since then.

Kira and I made our way through the crowd, speaking to a few people along the way, before finally reaching Brin and Leni. They were still holding hands, their cheeks flushed, their eyes dancing with joy.

"Congratulations," I said, giving them each a kiss on the cheek.

"Thank you," Brin said, flashing a dazzling smile at Leni.

Kira gave each of them a hug. "I'm so happy for you both."

"I couldn't imagine two people more perfect for each other," I said. "It's about time you two got married."

Leni laughed. "Brin was resistant for a long time, but I finally convinced her to marry me."

Brin waved her comment away. "I wasn't resistant, we were just busy!"

"Sure, that's what it was." Leni rolled her eyes with a smile.

"Excuse me if I was hesitant to get married after being forced to be betrothed to this man for so long," Brin said, nudging me with her elbow.

I laughed. "Oh, so now it's my fault?"

"Ignore her," Leni said. "We wouldn't have met at all if not for you."

Slade rested a hand on his younger sister's shoulder. "We're all very happy that it worked out this way."

We chatted for another few minutes before Brin and

Leni were called over to talk to someone else, leaving the three of us alone in our corner of the garden.

"You and I are officially family now," I said to Slade.

He wrapped one of his thick arms around my shoulder. "We've been family since Kira first brought us together."

Kira leaned against me with a smile. "And this is why we don't need a wedding."

"As usual, you're right," I said, kissing her on the cheek.

No, we didn't need a wedding. As Slade said, we were a family, bound to each other, heart and soul, our destinies entwined from our first breaths to the day we would leave this world. And in a few years, we'd have one more addition to that family. I, for one, couldn't wait.

41

SLADE

TEN YEARS LATER

I stared down at the bundle in my arms, taking in her perfection. Her skin was smooth, soft, and dark—not quite as dark as mine, but close. She had my dark hair too, although not very much of it yet. Her eyes were hazel though, like her mother's.

Kira watched me rocking little Sora from the doorway for a moment. "Well, there's no doubt she's your blood. She looks just like you."

I grinned as my daughter stared up at me with her big eyes. Before little Sora was born, we'd had no idea who had sired her. I had to admit I'd been thrilled seeing that she was mine, since I'd always wanted children. "She has my skin and hair, yes, but her beauty is all yours."

"Let's hope she has your calm temperament too."

Sora opened her mouth and let out a piercing wail in

response, making both of us laugh. Even when she was crying, she was cute somehow.

"It's probably time to feed her again," Kira said.

She settled in the rocking chair in one corner of the nursery and got all her pillows and blankets together, while I pressed a kiss to Sora's forehead. When Kira was ready, I handed her our daughter so she could begin nursing.

"Do you need anything?" I asked as they settled in.

"I don't think so, but thank you."

I nodded and relaxed in one of the other chairs with a sense of quiet contentment. I'd once wanted a simple life as a blacksmith in a small town with a wife and children. My life had ended up anything but simple, but somehow it turned out even better than I'd expected. I had a woman I loved more than I could ever imagine, three men who were like brothers to me, and a purpose that fulfilled me—and now my life was truly complete with the birth of our daughter.

Auric popped his head in the room. "The delegation from the Fire Realm has arrived."

"Thanks for letting me know," Kira said. The Fire Realm was in a dispute with the Water Realm over trade rights, and they wanted Kira to mediate. "Please tell them I'll be down in a few minutes."

He nodded. "Can I get you anything?"

Kira smiled at him. "No, thank you."

All of Kira's mates were eager to help out. With four fathers, Sora would never be short on love or attention, that was certain. Each man had already shown that they loved her as their own, and I didn't mind them sharing in the fatherly duties. Someday Sora would be the next ascendant with her own set of mates, and we would be there to train and guide her.

When Sora was finished, I took her from Kira again. "I'll put her to bed."

"Are you sure?" Kira asked.

I patted Sora on her back and got a good burp in response. "Yes. Go meet with the ambassadors and nobles. You know I hate that stuff anyway."

"Trust me, it's not my favorite either, but unfortunately it's necessary." She touched Sora's tiny nose, then gave me a kiss. "Thank you."

"It's my pleasure."

Kira straightened her clothes, drew herself up, and prepared to be a leader again. She worked hard, and our advisers had suggested that Kira get other women to nurse the baby and watch over her, but she'd refused. She wanted to raise Sora herself, and I sensed it was especially important to her after what happened with her own parents. The other men and I supported her as much as possible in both of her roles as the Silver Dragon and a mother. I knew there were times when it would be rough, but I was confident she could balance both, and we'd help her however we could.

After Kira left the room I changed Sora, then hummed a nursery rhyme my mother had sung to me and my sisters when we were little. When Sora's eyes drooped, I set her down in her bassinet. The future leader of the Dragons let out a big yawn and farted at the same time, making me laugh.

Yes, this life could be messy, complicated, and dangerous, but it was perfect.

42

REVEN

TWENTY YEARS LATER

W hile I leaned against the tree, Sora picked up the five small knives and tested their weight. Her little brow furrowed, while her dark hair blew in the breeze, and I waited in case she had any questions. When she was satisfied with the blades, she spun toward the target and threw them one by one. Each one hit the bullseye, her aim perfect, her throw confident.

I couldn't help but grin, my chest bursting with pride. "Nice job."

"Thanks, Dad." She did a little bounce and ran over to the target to yank the knives out.

Sora might not be my child by blood, but there was no doubt she was my daughter. I'd never wanted kids or imagined I would have them, but now I couldn't picture my life without her in it. Naturally I was her favorite dad because

I'd taught her all the fun stuff. How to throw knives. How to sneak about without being heard. How to pick locks. Kira joked that I was a bad influence, but I argued these were all things our daughter would need one day. No matter how safe we tried to make the world, there would always be problems the Dragons had to handle, and I wanted Sora to be prepared for anything.

"Take five steps back and try it again," I told her.

She nodded and did what I asked, with all the seriousness of a very determined ten-year-old. These training sessions were my favorite time of the day. I rotated with the others, each one of us claiming a few hours with the ascendant. Jasin taught her combat and war strategy, Auric taught her diplomacy and history, and Slade taught her how to build things. The rest of the time she spent with her tutors, playing with other kids living at the palace, or with Kira to learn about her future role as a Dragon.

Silver wings spread overhead, drawing our attention to the sky. "Mom's back!" Sora squealed.

The Silver Dragon circled down and landed beside us, and Sora ran over and wrapped her arms around Kira's neck. Kira nuzzled her scaled head against her daughter, before transforming into a human again. She'd been visiting the Earth Realm with Slade and Jasin after reports of shades in the area. I looked her over quickly, checking for signs she'd been in combat, but saw none.

"How did it go?" I asked.

She stretched her neck and shoulders. "We didn't see

any shades, but Jasin and Slade are patrolling the area for another few days to make sure. What have you two been doing?"

"Training," I said.

"Look what Dad taught me," Sora said. She grabbed the five knives and launched them into the air, juggling them with skill.

Kira arched an eyebrow at me. "Wow. That looks...dangerous."

"Oh, Mom," Sora said, rolling her eyes as she caught all five knives. "It's fine."

"She's a natural," I said. "And besides, if she gets hurt, she'll heal it quick enough."

Sora had already come into her healing powers thanks to the Life Goddess, who'd blessed Sora early as a gift for us freeing her. It already looked like Sora would surpass her mother in magic, as she could heal anyone she touched and cause plants to grow. Animals loved her too, naturally. I could only imagine how powerful she would be once she received the magic of her future mates too—although the thought of her with mates was too terrifying to think about just yet.

"Just be careful," Kira said, while stroking Sora's hair.

"We always are. Don't worry." I wrapped my arms around Kira and kissed her, while Sora squirmed away and said, "ew." She danced off across the courtyard, finding something else to entertain herself with, while I held her mother in my arms. "I missed you."

"I missed you too," she said, leaning against me. "Come to my room tonight, after she's asleep."

"I was already planning on it," I said, kissing her again.

43

KIRA

THIRTY YEARS LATER

Storm clouds rolled over the garden, crackling with the promise of what was to come. Any moment now the rain would begin, lightning would strike, and my daughter would be blessed by the Gods.

"Will it hurt?" Sora asked me, as she had done many times while she was growing up.

"Only for a moment," I said.

It was her twentieth birthday, and today her mates would be chosen. It had been over thirty years since that day for me, but I still remembered it well. Enva had appeared to me for the first time and then I'd been struck by lightning, doused in rain, whipped by wind, and had fallen in the mud. Now I knew it had been the four Gods blessing me with their elements, but back then I'd been confused, especially when I wasn't injured afterward. Sora, at least, was a lot better prepared.

"Don't worry. You can handle it." I smoothed her dark hair and gazed into her hazel eyes. She was so beautiful, a young woman with so much strength and such a good heart, embodying all the best things of each of my mates. "I'm so proud of you. I know you're going to do great things."

She drew in a breath and stood a little taller. "Thanks, Mom. I have a big legacy to live up to, but I'll do my best."

"I know you will." I pressed a kiss to her forehead, and then I moved back to where my mates were waiting off to the side, giving Sora some space. Though we'd all aged by thirty years since we'd first met, they were still just as handsome, and our love had only grown stronger over the years.

Slade paced back and forth relentlessly. "How are we supposed to just stand here and do nothing while our daughter is hit by lightning?"

"The better question is, how are we supposed to stand here and do nothing, knowing her mates are going to be chosen today?" Jasin asked.

"She'll be fine," Reven said, though I noticed his face was looking a bit pale and his brows were furrowed.

"Yes, she will," Auric said, as he nervously ran a hand through his golden hair. "She's prepared for this her whole life."

"I'm not worried," I said. "Most women only have one overprotective father. She has four to watch over her."

"We're not overprotective," Slade said, even though he was the worst of them.

Jasin scowled. "All I know is that these mates of hers had

better treat her right, or they're going to have to deal with me."

"The Gods did a good job of choosing all of you," I said. "We have to trust they'll find the perfect men for Sora too."

Auric tilted his head with a thoughtful look on his face. "If I recall correctly, none of us were perfect when we first met you, but we grew into the roles. We'll have to allow her mates to do the same."

"And if they don't, I'll take them out and dispose of the bodies where no one can find them," Reven said with a dark grin.

I shook my head. "No one is taking them out. Besides, Sora can handle herself. You've all made sure of that."

Sora crossed her arms and called out, "How long am I supposed to wait?"

"I'm sure it will be soon," I yelled back.

She huffed and gazed up at the sky as rain began to pelt down on her face. It was hard to believe she was all grown up now and ready to become the next Silver Dragon, or whatever color she ended up as. We'd spent the last thirty years trying to bring peace to the four Realms so her transition would be as easy as possible, and I hoped Enva, Doran, and Nysa would be proud of all we'd accomplished. The four Realms governed themselves independently, and we'd prevented many wars from starting between them over the years. The elementals and humans lived in relative harmony, and when shades crept out of the Realm of the Dead, we swiftly dealt with them. The world had changed dramatically, and I had no idea what challenges Sora would face as she took over as its guardian, but I was confident she could handle them.

As for us? My mates and I were ready to step back and begin our retirement. We'd help train Sora and her mates, of course, but our time as peacekeepers, mediators, and warriors was at an end. I had to admit, I was excited for a long, well-deserved break.

Lightning streaked down from the sky and struck Sora, making her entire body go rigid, her arms spread wide as if she was embracing it. Wind wrapped around her, lifting her into the air, while rain soaked through her clothes and mud splashed against her skin. My mates tensed beside me and I felt their anxiety and worry through the bond as we all watched. I'd never admit it out loud to them, but I was worried too. How could I not be? Sora's life was about to change forever. But I also had faith in our daughter and knew she would find her way, just like we did.

It was time for a new set of Dragons to rise.

ABOUT THE AUTHOR

New York Times Bestselling Author Elizabeth Briggs writes unputdownable romance across genres with bold heroines and fearless heroes. She graduated from UCLA with a degree in Sociology and has worked for an international law firm, mentored teens in writing, and volunteered with dog rescue groups. Now she's a full-time geek who lives in Los Angeles with her husband and a pack of fluffy dogs.

Visit Elizabeth's website: www.elizabethbriggs.net

ALSO BY ELIZABETH BRIGGS

Future Lost